D0546838

Hansard lifted his head and gazed down at her. Emma saw such concern and love in his eyes that she felt humbled. He did love her, even if he didn't know it yet. A man didn't feel that desperate anxiety for a mere friend. She melted against the warm, hard wall of his chest as his arms held her safe in an iron grip.

Her choking laughter turned to a whimper in her throat as she met his gaze. For a long moment they looked at each other as if hypnotized. Emma's lips trembled open, just as his head lowered. . . .

By Joan Smith
Published by Fawcett Books:

AN
INFAMOUS
PROPOSAL

Joan Smith

FAWCETT CREST • NEW YORK

A Fawcett Crest Book
Published by Ballantine Books
Copyright © 1997 by Joan Smith

http://www.randomhouse.com

Library of Congress Catalog Card Number: 96-97059

ISBN 0-449-22552-6

Manufactured in the United States of America

First Edition: January 1997

10 9 8 7 6 5 4 3 2 1

Chapter One

Emma Capehart sat staring glumly at the letter before her. She had been receiving threatening letters for the past eighteen months; now the ax had fallen. She had read it till the words were engraved on her mind, her spirits sinking lower at each perusal.

Dear Lady Capehart—Emma: (Papa was impressed by the late Sir John's baronetcy and insisted on using that "Lady.")

Now that you are out of mourning and will be gradually returning into Society, we can no longer put off finding you a more reliable chaperone than Miss Foxworth. You are still too young, at two and twenty, to manage your own affairs, and I fear that Miss Foxworth will be but little help to you. Your aunt Hildegarde has kindly agreed to remove to Whitehern to stay with you until you have made another match. I need hardly say this is a grave imposition on her goodwill, and indeed she will be sorely missed at home.

She will require a week's time to prepare. Let us know when it will be convenient for you to send your carriage for her. See that you give her a room without drafts—her rheumatism is at her again. You will speak to your housekeeper about your aunt's diet. Any sort of pork is slow poison to her.

1

Two closely written sheets outlined the arrangements that must be made to harbor Aunt Hildegarde. Emma paid little heed to any of them. She was determined not to have this Tartar foisted on her. Hildegarde Milmont had made life a hell at home for seventeen years. The best part of marrying John had been escaping her. Perhaps that was why she had married him. . . .

At times Emma felt guilty for not grieving her late husband's death more deeply. She had loved John, hadn't she? Yet there was no denying that once she had overcome the initial shock of his passing, she had felt something akin to relief. How could it be possible? The happiest years of her life were those since marrying John. But she had soon sensed something lacking—some passion, or romance. John had been a good deal older than she, of course. She had never had any other beaux to compare him with.

Since his death she had enjoyed being her own mistress, ordering the house and meals to her own whim. She had been looking forward to the greater freedom of dinner parties and assemblies and beaux when her mourning period was up. And now the fateful letter had arrived. She knew as surely as she knew her own name that Aunt Hildegarde would come and deprive her of those treats. She would arrive with her possets and shawls, her pills and tisanes, and turn the house into a hospital. One was tempted to say Hildegard enjoyed ill health, but it wasn't true. She didn't enjoy anything except nagging.

No *parti* would pass muster with Hildegarde, if he were pleasing to Emma. From the bishop of Canterbury to the Prince Regent, the inhabitants of this world were just not up to Hildegarde's high standards. It was odd that this misanthrope should be so determined to see the human race perpetuated; yet the one thing that brought a light to her faded eyes was making matches and having those matches bear fruit. What a husband Hildegarde would choose for her! Some teetotaling complainer like herself.

Emma looked around the handsome Blue Saloon, furnished in expensive good taste, and sighed as her mind roved over the recent past. John had come to visit relatives near her home in Wiltshire. He had seen her in church, arranged an introduction the next day, fallen in love with her, and married her within three months. Not even Hildegarde could find a fault in him. Indeed, there was no fault to find. John was as near perfect as a man could be. So why had the joy faded from their marriage? Perhaps if she had had a child her life would have been fuller.

But even if she'd had children, Papa would have insisted she have a strict chaperone after John's death. The only way of escaping it was to find another husband at once. Where would she find such another jewel as John? He gave her whatever she wanted—nothing was too extravagant for his Emma. More gowns and bonnets and jewelry than she had ever had in her whole life. The only thing he denied her was the thing she craved most—a Season in London.

Her family had no connections there who could introduce her to the ton. John's relatives were older aunts, who did not go into Society. What she required, then, was a husband who spent the Season in London. One gentleman was at the top of her list—her neighbor and John's good friend, Nicholas Arden, Lord Hansard, of Waterdown Hall. He and Emma had carried on an innocent flirtation from the first day they met.

"You have shown us all the way, John," he had

said, taking Emma's hand and lifting it to his lips. It was the first time a gentleman had ever done that to Emma. She had been shocked, and thrilled to the marrow of her bones. "Where are the rest of us to find such a jewel as your Emma?"

Nick played the gallant at the local balls, always making a point of standing up with her for the waltzes. John did not waltz. When Nick went up to London, he brought back the latest novels and magazines to her. She felt fairly sure he would offer for her, now that she was free. What she had not decided was whether she would accept him. He was handsome and gallant, and of course wealthy. It would be a great match in every way. Even Hildegarde, who shared her brother's love of a title, would not find much wrong with it. But then Hildegarde didn't know about Mrs. Pettigrew. Emma had already decided she would insist Nick turn off his mistress if she married him.

The greatest hurdle was the timing of his offer. If she could get a proposal from him very soon, she could write to Papa that she had received an unexceptionable offer. An offer from Lord Hansard would obviate inconveniencing Hildegarde, who disliked travel. Papa wrote the truth when he said that her coming was a duty and a sacrifice. And Lord Hansard's offer need not be accepted. . . .

Nicholas was stopping by that very evening to bring her some silk from London. How she looked forward to putting off her mourning gowns! Papa had insisted on black for the entire eighteen months. To switch to half mourning after twelve months would have been an insult not only to John, but to God. Perhaps Nick would offer for her this very evening, now that her mourning period was over.

Her woolgathering was interrupted by Miss Foxworth.

"What has your papa to say, Emma?" she asked, lifting her eyes from her novel. They were faded blue eyes, set in a pale face, surrounded by rusty hair bound up in an unbecoming lace cap. Miss Foxworth was a poor relation of John's from the neighborhood. She had removed to Whitehern at the time of John's death. At fifty years, Miriam Foxworth had given up any notion of elegance. She lived in a wonderful make-believe world of put-upon heroines, wicked villains, and heroes who made all right in the end.

"He wants Aunt Hildegarde to come to stay with me," Emma said.

"Oh dear! She is the one you don't care for, is she not?"

"She is very strict."

"Pity." Even as Miss Foxworth spoke, her eyes returned to the page. She looked up again, a frown puckering her brow. "Will she want me to leave? So kind of you to have me. Of course, I could always go back to Cousin Millicent and George." These cousins did not live in such high style as Lady Capehart.

"Of course you must stay," Emma said.

Miss Foxworth resumed her reading, and Emma went back to her planning. Emma's besetting sin was impetuosity. Within the twinkling of a bedpost, she had decided she must wring an offer from Nicholas tonight when he called. She rose suddenly, her mind made up.

"I'm going upstairs, Miss Foxworth. Call me when Lord Hansard arrives."

"Very well, dear," Miss Foxworth replied, without looking up.

Emma darted abovestairs to prepare a toilette to seduce Lord Hansard into an offer of marriage. She had not yet taken her colored gowns out of camphor. She regretted that she was still wearing black, yet it was becoming to her. For evening wear she had chosen a gown cut low enough at the bodice to be fashionable without being indiscreet. It clung to the graceful curves of her lithe, young body and provided a dramatic contrast to her creamy complexion. Her hair was as black as her gown and of the same silken texture. Lamplight brought a flicker of iridescence to the smooth waves drawn back from a high forehead. Her wide-set eyes were the stormy gray green of the Atlantic on an overcast day and looked as bottomless. The severity of black hair and gray eyes was lightened by a small nose, slightly retroussé to give her an insouciant air. A set of full lips added a touch of the coquette.

It had come as a surprise to Emma to hear from John that she was beautiful. Aunt Hildegarde had convinced her she had a "common" look, by which she meant, perhaps, that Emma was attractive to gentlemen. Nicholas had certainly seemed to think so. His attentions had not diminished at John's death, but they had changed subtly in character. He was too wellbred to flirt with a grieving widow. He had come as often as before to offer his assistance in estate matters.

Emma, having gone at seventeen years directly from her papa's home to her husband's, was a perfect greenhead in some areas. She hardly knew what procedure should be followed when she made a new match. As she was a widow, would the offer come directly to herself? Miss Foxworth was nominally her chaperon, but Nicholas knew that Emma ruled the roost. She didn't want Nicholas to confer with her papa on the engagement. That would lend it a seriousness and certainty she wanted to avoid. Hildegarde would rush the news directly to the journals. A private understanding between Nick and herself was what Emma wanted. Then if it broke down, it could be kept a secret from the locals. She would tell Papa she was considering the offer. Letters might be exchanged for months on such a weighty matter.

But first she had to get her offer. If he didn't come up to scratch, could she not suggest it herself? It was not unusual for a lady's papa or guardian to suggest a match to an eligible gentleman. With no papa at hand, who else could do it but herself? As these thoughts ran through her mind, there was a tap at the door. Mary, the downstairs maid, peeped in.

"Lord Hansard is belowstairs, ma'am," she said.

"Thank you, Mary."

Emma set down her brush and gave herself a last look in the mirror. Her eyes glowed with excitement at the daring of her plan. A rosy flush bloomed on her cheeks as she lifted the perfume bottle and dabbed the stopper behind her ears. Then she took up a cashmere shawl and went down to meet Lord Hansard.

Chapter Two

Upon Emma's entrance Lord Hansard rose and turned to study her. He was always surprised at how lovely she looked and how unlike a grieving widow. Had she ever cared for John at all, or had it been creampot love? The young, undowered daughter of a small gentleman farmer had done pretty well for herself to nab Sir John Capehart. Hansard knew something of Emma's origins, knew that the lady had brought nothing to the marriage except her pretty face and her pert, encroaching manner.

One would have expected such a wife to be devoted to her husband, yet Emma, while avoiding outright impropriety, had always behaved in a cavalier fashion to John. More than half his own fault, of course. He had treated the chit like the queen of Sheba. Upon her husband's death she had observed the proprieties almost to excess. Eighteen months of unrelieved black was not required. Black was, however, very becoming to the young widow. Nicholas sensed that below the black gowns and downcast eyes, a flirt was impatient to escape.

With her mourning period coming to an end, she hadn't wasted a second to send off to London for colored silks. She could cut a wider swath in Society now that she had John's estate and fortune at her back. Very likely she intended to invade London in the autumn Little Season and nab herself a title. She would have scant difficulty, what with that face and fortune. She could have her pick, even nab a title.

"Lady Capehart," he said, sketching a graceful bow.

"You're very formal this evening, Nick," she replied. Her full lips fell naturally into that fetching pout.

Emma regarded her caller with a more assessing eye than formerly, measuring him as a potential husband. She harbored a secret passion for tall, dark gentlemen. John had been of medium height, with brown hair. Lord Hansard topped six feet, with an inch to spare. A velvet jacket the shade of brandy clung like a plaster to his broad shoulders. An oriental topaz the same color rested in the folds of his immaculate cravat. His jet hair was cropped close to his head à la Titus. Her eyes swept quickly over his body, then back to study his face. His lean, clever face, swarthy from wind and sun, was not so much handsome as lively and intelligent. Those dark eyes saw too much. She sometimes felt he could see right through her.

"You must blame my formality on Whitehall," he said. "I've been to Parliament to consult with our member on county business." He noticed that, although Emma was now a large landowner, she was not curious enough to inquire what local business had taken him to Whitehall.

"Did you remember my silk?" she asked.

"Certainly I did. I gave it to Soames."

The silk evinced an interest that was sorely lacking in more serious matters. "I would like to see it. I hope you didn't get a dark green, Nick. It washes my color out entirely. I wanted a pale, minty shade."

Nicholas called Soames, and the parcel was brought in for inspection.

"Lovely!" she exclaimed, fingering the rich stuff.

"I've already chosen a pattern from *La Belle Assemblée*. I might have known I could trust your judgment," she added, with one of her careless smiles that brought a dimple to the corner of her lips. Just so had she deigned to compliment John when he spoiled her.

"Would you care for a glass of wine, Lord Hansard?" Miss Foxworth offered. The widow, of course, was too wrapped up in her new silk to tend to the civilities.

"A cup of tea would be welcome," he replied, and Miss Foxworth ordered it.

While they took their tea, Hansard amused the ladies with tales of London fashions and gossip. He had met Lord Byron at a party and gave a much expurgated account of the poet's romantic doings.

"How I should love to meet him!" Emma sighed.

"If he knew it, he would be here in a flash," Hansard said, not entirely facetiously. What a meeting that would be, between those two beautiful, spoiled young darlings. The reverberations would be heard in America.

Emma smiled at this confirmation of her desirability. Hansard, watching her, noticed that she seemed especially excited this evening. Her dark eyes sparkled with some suppressed emotion. Was it the silk that brought that gleam to her eyes, or was it his London tales? She used to pester John to take her to London.

When the tea was finished, he rose to take his leave. Emma said, "Would you mind coming into the study for a moment, Nick? There's something I would like to ask you." Away from Miss Foxworth she hoped some romance would develop. It seemed hard to crop out into a proposal with no preliminary flirtation.

"She's off to London and wants me to sponsor her in Society," he said to himself, and hardly knew what he would reply. Thank God the Season was winding down. He could put her off until the fall Little Season. It would be difficult to refuse outright, but he had no intention of making himself responsible for her. Perhaps he could recommend a socially prominent chaperon. Some noble dames in straitened circumstances enjoyed the Season without expense by sponsoring wealthy parvenues. He bowed to Miss Foxworth and followed Emma into John's study.

Emma had set the stage for the proposal. The fire was lit, with two chairs drawn before it, but Hansard hardly glanced at all this. His eyes moved to the desk, where the estate ledger was open. Earlier Emma had been working on the accounts. Emma, surprisingly, had a head for numbers. He glanced at the neat rows of figures that filed down the page in enviable order. She even used John's abacus, a tool Nicholas found confusing himself. One could not fault Emma on her management. Perhaps he had been a little hard on her. All pretty ladies were interested in their gowns.

"Have you encountered some problem, Emma?" he asked, with a note of genuine concern.

Emma moved toward the grate. She sat in one of the pair of rose bergère chairs drawn up before the fire. A decanter of wine and two glasses sat on a side table nearby.

She caught his note of concern and adopted a worried little frown that John could never resist. "A widow has many problems," she said on a weary sigh.

"Especially a young, charming widow," he said, in his usual chivalrous manner. That earned him a

11

smile. "You can always rely on me, Emma," he said. "I am at your disposal. What is it that troubles you?"

She indicated the empty chair, and he sat down. Her dainty white hand, hovering close to his, seemed to ask for reassurance. He seized her fingers and squeezed gently. He was relieved to notice she still wore the wedding band John had given her.

"It is being alone, trying to run this estate. Now that my mourning period is over, I—" She looked helplessly at him from below a fan of long lashes.

It is to be London! he thought, stiffening. "You are thinking of making a match?" he asked, his voice thinning in disapproval at her haste.

Emma construed his stiffening manner as jealousy and was convinced he loved her. "It would make my life easier, Nicholas," she said softly.

"And mine," he replied, thinking of the many estate matters he had been handling for her since John's death. As John's closest friend and neighbor, he had felt some responsibility for his widow, and she had never hesitated to seek his help.

Her eyelashes moved flirtatiously. So the idea didn't come as a surprise to him! She wished that he would speak first. Now that the moment had come, she was strangely loath to put her proposition to him.

"Have you anything to suggest?" she asked, tightening her hold on his fingers.

He gazed into her eyes, trying to read her mood, then said, "A good marriage is the obvious solution."

She breathed a sigh of relief and directed a coquettish smile at him. "I am happy to see we think alike, Nick," she said. Odd that he chose this promising moment to withdraw his fingers. Was it her wedding band that had put him off? Or was he going to rise and take her in his arms? A warmth invaded her, then faded to disappointment as she realized he was just reaching to pour them a glass of wine.

"A toast?" she suggested, when he handed her a glass.

His jaw stiffened. Really the chit had no finesse, to be toasting her freedom, as if it were a triumph to have buried a husband. He lifted his glass and said coldly, "This would be to the termination of your mourning period, I collect?"

She made a moue with her full lips, then laughed forgivingly. "That is not very romantic, sir!"

"I fear I am not at all romantical, Emma. Do you expect me to rejoice that you plan to run off to London and set the ton on its ear with your husband hunting?"

"London! Oh, but you misunderstand me. I want to marry *you*!"

Chapter Three

The words came out without thinking. Nick had misunderstood, and she was just setting him right, in her usual frank manner. She watched as his hand moved convulsively. Wine sloshed over the glass's rim and onto his cream satin waistcoat. Three small red dots spread to form larger pink circles. "Is—is that not what you meant?" she asked in confusion. "I thought—I just assumed—"

He stared at her a moment, speechless with anger. When he found voice, Emma wished he had not. "Marry *you*?" he asked, his voice high with disbelief and heavy with irony. "Upon my word, you take a good deal for granted, Lady Capehart."

"But you said—"

"I said you could count on me for any little matter about the estate that requires a man's attention. My offer falls a good deal short of marriage."

Emma found it hard to tell whether he was more astonished or outraged. She felt the sting of deep humiliation. When she realized her error, her humiliation was rapidly followed by a flash of anger. "There's no need to pull your ears back like an angry mare, Hansard. You needn't think I love you!"

"Then why have you just proposed marriage to me?"

"Because—because Papa is going to send Aunt Hildegarde," she said, and clenched her lips to hold in a surge of tears, which were due more to Hansard's rebuke than to the threat of Hildegarde. Anger and shame burned like acid inside her.

"And you are actually scatterbrained enough to marry only to avoid an aunt's visit? I fear you and I have a vastly different view of marriage, ma'am. I don't consider it a prank or trick to avoid some minor unpleasantness. When I marry it will be to a lady I love and respect."

"Are you saying you don't respect me?" she shot back. All fear of tears vanished, leaving behind undiluted anger.

"I find it hard to respect a lady who would offer for a gentleman who has given no indication of interest in her."

"I didn't offer! I thought that was what you meant! What else should a lady think when you are always underfoot. You just said I could rely on you, that you were always at my disposal."

"That was mere courtesy," he snapped, wincing at that "always underfoot." She was always summoning him!

She tossed her head defiantly. "Is that what you call it? In any case, it would be an excellent match. Whitehern and your estate run side by side. I doubt you will find any lady better dowered or less demanding."

"I see no reason to suppose you would be less demanding as a wife than as a neighbor. And you have omitted the other rather important factor. I don't love you."

She sniffed to cover her shame. But the two red flags burning on her cheeks betrayed her agitation. "Love has nothing to do with it. I had in mind a marriage of convenience." This was not true, but her self-respect required some bolstering. She couldn't let

15

him walk away with the idea that she loved him. Indeed, at that moment she despised him thoroughly.

A gasp of astonishment hung on the air. "This goes from bad to worse!" he charged. "You are saying you don't even like me, but you are willing—nay—eager to have me. I can only assume the advantage of adding my estate to yours is the real motive behind this extraordinary suggestion."

"I only mentioned that because I thought it might appeal to your—vanity," she said, unhappy with the last word, but unable to think of a better one. "I am not in the least eager to have you. I considered you marginally better than Aunt Hildegarde—and *she* is horrid." She assumed an air of dignity and said, "I see now that I was mistaken. We should not suit in the least."

"That is something we can agree on." He rose stiffly and set down his glass. The astonishing, tumultuous nature of their meeting left him in a state of bewilderment. Yet despite all, he still felt some responsibility for Emma. Her performance that evening showed him she was in dire need of guidance. He braced himself to speak once more. "If you wish to marry, Lady Capehart, I suggest you set about it in the regular way. This sort of forward behavior will only disgust any gentleman of taste and refinement."

"So I assume, when it even disgusted you," she retorted childishly. "And how can I proceed in the regular way?" she asked angrily. "I have no one to arrange the matter for me. I cannot see Miss Foxworth handling it any better than I did myself."

"It is hard to see how she could have done worse! You have a father—"

"We will leave Papa out of this, if you please. He is miles away."

"I'm sure he would be willing to come, if necessary."

"Yes, with Aunt Hildegarde. I have told you that is precisely what I wish to avoid." Emma was now eager to terminate the visit. She rose and said, "How much do I owe you for the silk?"

He handed her the bill. She went to her cash box and extracted the sum. "Keep the change," she said grandly. Nick counted out a few pennies and handed them to her with a lowering look.

"Thank you, Lord Hansard. I appreciate your fetching it for me," she said. "I shan't bother you in future. I didn't realize I had been imposing so wretchedly on your good nature. You should have mentioned it sooner."

"I was happy to do it, Emma," he said, in a gentler tone. "Indeed, I did not mean to imply I resented any little assistance I may have rendered in the past. I hope you will call me if—"

Her sharp reply cut through his pretty speech like a knife through sausage. "You are too kind," she said, but her cold tone said there would be icicles in hell before she applied to his kindness again. She lifted her chin and glared. "Good night, Lord Hansard, and, once more, thank you for your kindness."

He hovered at the doorway, not wanting to leave with bad feelings between them, but not knowing what to say that would not set her off again. "Must we really begin 'lord' and 'ladying' each other, after all this time, Emma?"

"You're the one who called me Lady Capehart first."

"What you suggest would not do, you know."

"Truth to tell, I hadn't the least wish to marry you. I thought if I could tell Papa I had an offer, Hildegarde might not come. It need not have come to an actual wedding."

This piece of chicanery did much to rekindle Hansard's ire. He was to be jilted into the bargain! "Good evening, Lady Capehart," he said through stiff lips.

Emma watched as he went out and slammed the door behind him. She had never seen such an eloquent back. Every inch of his broad shoulders derided her presumption. She buried her face in her hands and uttered a strangled cry of vexation. What a wretched botch she had made of it! She shouldn't have blurted it out so suddenly. Nick had no interest in her whatsoever. All these months she had been nothing to him but a pest. He hadn't meant any of those compliments he used to shower on her. They were just to please John. Worst of all, the whole neighborhood would soon know what an egregious ass she had made of herself. She flew out the door after him.

Lord Hansard was still in the hallway, just donning his curled beaver as she arrived, breathless, at the front door. She dismissed the butler, who stood ready to see Hansard out, and spoke to Nicholas in a low tone.

"A gentleman, I believe, does not boast of his conquests," she said, peering up at him with a beseeching look. Her bottom lip began trembling. Her childish expression made him regret his harsh attack. Emma was still young after all.

He shook his head and gave a rueful sigh. "Don't worry, Emma, I shan't boast of this night's work. I fear we neither of us appeared at our best. Let us forget it happened and continue friends."

She studied him for signs of irony or, worse, laughter. She saw only a worried gaze. "Thank you, Nicholas," she said in a small voice.

He opened the door and left. His traveling carriage

18

and team of four were standing outside, as he had planned to remain only a short while. As he was driven home through the darkness, it was the image of the worried young face at the door and the small, soft voice that went with him. Emma had often complained of her aunt Hildegarde, but it seemed impossible that Emma had proposed to him only to avoid the visit. No, that visit had been a mere pretext and so had that claim of a marriage of convenience. The fact was, she wanted to marry him. Beneath the annoyance and surprise, he felt a little glow of pride or pleasure. It wasn't every evening that a gentleman received an offer of marriage from a beautiful young heiress.

Of course, it was incredibly farouche of her to have put the offer to him herself, but as an offer, it was hardly offensive. At three and thirty Hansard was at an age when he often thought of marriage, but he planned to choose his own bride—and she wouldn't be a spoiled beauty of low breeding. He didn't love Emma, nor she him. She just wanted to make a good match. His title was but another step up her ladder of self-advancement. He had thought she would head straight for London. Perhaps she preferred to tackle Society from the unassailable position of Lord Hansard's lady.

By the time he reached home, he half regretted his rough refusal. His teasing manner with her in the past, always when John was in the room to remove any air of impropriety, must have misled her. He might have let the chit down more gently. Emma really was very pretty and still green as grass. She'd marry the first handsome fortune hunter who came along—and saddle him with an unsavory neighbor.

The least he could do, for both their sakes, was import a suitable match for her. His mind sped over cousins and connections who were on the lookout for a well-dowered bride. It would be nice to have, say, Cousin James, at Whitehern. Lord James Philmore, his mama's nephew, was in need of a fortune. Emma might not balk at James's empty pockets when his face was so pleasing and his papa was an earl. It would raise her position in Society and assure her a Season in London.

Happy that he had hit on a solution, he wrote a note off to Lord James that very evening.

At Whitehern Emma stewed in embarrassment and anger. How could she have made such a fool of herself? How could Nick have let her? He had always seemed to like her, but beneath his suave manners, he had been laughing at her, despising her. "Marry *you*?" he had exclaimed, as if she were a yahoo. And after it all she was still faced with Aunt Hildegarde's coming.

"Where is Miss Foxworth?" she asked Soames, when he came to remove her silk.

"She went to bed with the sniffles, madam. I fear she is coming down with a cold."

"A cold!" Emma exclaimed, and smiled in delight.

The very thing! Aunt Hildegarde, that hypochondriac par excellence, would never visit a house infected with disease. Miss Foxworth's cold must escalate to influenza or even pneumonia. When the pneumonia was conquered, say in a month, Aunt Hildegarde would hear that there was a smallpox scare in the village. Emma suddenly had a dozen ideas to put off the dreaded visit. Why had she thought she needed horrid Nicholas to rescue her? It had become too easy to send for him in all her little troubles. That was over now. She was a mature lady. She would look after herself. No more running to him with every little problem.

And if Hildegarde insisted on coming despite all, she would find her niece a changed person. Why should Lady Capehart take orders from Hildegarde in her own house? She was mistress here. It was time she began to act the role.

But when she was tucked under the counterpane that night, she felt grave misgivings about her ability to face up to Hildegarde. She also still felt a rankling disappointment at Nick's blunt refusal. Did he not care for her even a little? How could she have been so mistaken about a thing like that? Ah well, no point shaving a pig. He was not interested, and she must find a new beau. Until she was safely shackled, the threat of visits from home would shadow her life.

Chapter Four

The next morning as he was going to his stable, Lord Hansard saw William Bounty riding through Emma's park toward Whitehern. Bounty was Emma's neighbor on the west side and a friend of both Emma and himself. What invested this unexceptionable gentleman with an unaccustomed aura of interest that morning was Emma's determination to marry. If she had sent for Bounty to put her offer to him, he would have her in a minute! From the first moment Bounty had clapped an eye on Emma, he had been in love with her. He was an older widower who made no secret that he wanted another wife, since his first one had not given him an heir, but only a daughter, now married.

A cynical smile curved Hansard's lips. Bounty would be disappointed to hear it was a marriage of convenience the widow was offering. Had she been serious about that? She hadn't mentioned it at first. Did she really think any man with blood in his veins could share a house with her under such terms? Whatever her faults she was an exquisite-looking woman. She would make a better mistress than a wife. Hansard had always thought those bewitching, self-serving smiles and dimples were wasted on John.

He had his mare saddled up for a tour of his tenant

farms, but as he discussed crops and herds and marling, he found his mind wandering back to Whitehern.

A little before noon he cut his business short and returned home. His eyes traveled west to the boundary of his land, with Emma's lush acres spreading enticingly beyond—excellent land, with a large herd of prime milchers grazing in the sunlight. If it were to join his own, it would be the finest spread in Sussex.

Hansard's housekeeper, Mrs. Denver, had been in Waterdown Hall as long as he could remember. She was a widowed distant cousin of small means. She didn't take her meals with Hansard, but in every other way, she was considered as family. She often took coffee with him after his meal to discuss household doings. She did so that day after lunch.

"I saw Bounty riding over to Whitehern this morning," he said, and looked for her reaction. "There was no announcement?" Emma's kitchen maid was keeping company with one of his footmen. If a wedding had been announced, the news would have reached Waterdown by now.

"What sort of announcement? You don't mean Lady Capehart is selling Whitehern! Oh, I would be sorry to lose her."

"No, I thought there might be a match in that quarter."

She looked at him in astonishment. "Surely not! She can do better than that. She will soon be snapped up, but it won't be William Bounty who gets her. I have often thought you and she might come to terms. It seemed a natural thing, the right thing," she said. "Time to settle down, milord."

He recognized this as a reference to Mrs. Pettigrew. This dasher had moved to the neighborhood three years before. As he had known her in London when she was under Lord Quarter's patronage, he had called on her a few times. Before long he realized the lady was interested in marriage. Since then his visits were limited to her large parties.

"Mrs. Pettigrew is a friend, nothing more."

Mrs. Denver spoke on of Emma, praising her good nature, her looks, and her fortune.

"She is certainly eligible," he agreed, with growing frustration. It was not only Mrs. Denver who realized Emma's eligibility. Every Benedict for miles around was aware of it. Emma realized it herself. She was chomping at the bit. "In fact, I posted a note to Lord James this very morning."

Mrs. Denver said, "Lady Capehart would like the noble connection, and you could keep an eye out to see that Lord James doesn't run amok." That addendum was a reminder that while Lord James was a handsome fellow, he was no serious one.

A moment later she said, "Is it her being a widow that you dislike?"

"Not in the least. Between ourselves, the lady is an idle, vain, provincial fribble. She has no interest in serious or cultural matters."

"She's young yet. You'll not find many bluestockings hereabouts," Mrs. Denver said, then spoke of household matters.

Nick felt dissatisfied after their chat. Was he being foolishly demanding in his requirements for a bride? Perhaps with training, Emma might do him proud after all. He ought to have taken time to think over her offer. "Lord, I sound like a lady!" he said to himself. But he had done right to reject her offer. A lady who proposed to a gentleman surely passed the bounds of acceptable behavior.

Still, he would drop in at Whitehern and apologize for his brusqueness the evening before. If Bounty had accepted her, she would be sure to fling it in his face. Hansard took a brace of partridge as an excuse. Since John's death he often took her game for her dinner. She had given him free shooting at Whitehern. That was generous of her. She really was a generous sort of girl.

At three o'clock that afternoon he posted over to Whitehern, where he was told that Lady Capehart had taken a book to the gazebo. It was a favorite spot of Emma's on a fine day. From the crest of the hill, she could see the road leading to London. Deeply engrossed in her book when Hansard passed, she didn't see him.

He came upon her unawares and stopped for a moment to gaze at her. Shafts of sunlight filtered through the vine-covered roof, sprinkling her head and shoulders with dancing beads of light. She was still dressed in black, but wore a violet shawl over her shoulders to soften the mourning effect. One finger played with her curls in an endearingly child-like manner. Surely this girl was too innocent to have made her offer out of self-interest. John's aging spaniel, Rusty, sat dozing at her feet. Rusty discerned the approach of an intruder and set up a spate of barking. Emma looked up to see who it was.

There was no ignoring the scowl that seized her mobile features. Her lips formed into a pout, and her chin lifted at a challenging angle.

"Nicholas," she said coolly, all childishness slipping from her. It was a hostile young lady who greeted him. But at least she hadn't called him "Lord Hansard" in that arctic way.

"Good day, Emma," he said, ignoring her mood. "I brought you some partridges for dinner. I left them with Soames. He told me I might find you here."

"A peace offering wasn't necessary, but I thank you."

He entered the gazebo uninvited and sat down on an uncomfortable wooden seat. "A lovely day," he said, glancing out at the sun-drenched park, dappled with shade from spreading elms and oak, with a sprinkling of copper beeches to add variety. In the near distance, the weathered brick of Whitehern rose impressively.

"Yes. Miss Foxworth has taken cold so I cannot drive out."

This mixture of propriety and self-interest was typical of Emma. He never knew quite what to make of her.

"I hope you had some callers to lighten the tedium of being alone?" he asked.

She leveled a stern gaze on him. "I don't find my own company tedious, Nicholas. If you find me boring, pray do not feel obliged to remain. You will be relieved to hear I have no commissions for you today."

Emma could be selfish, frustrating, flighty, and thoroughly annoying. She could also be charming, amusing, and generous. "I never find beautiful ladies tedious," he replied. "What I was trying to discover, in my roundabout way, was whether you had offered for Bounty. I saw him calling on you."

"That old snuff dipper!" After her first outburst, she took a few deep breaths to control her temper. It did not surprise Nick that she failed. When she spoke again, her voice held a wintry tinge of frost.

"No, I did not make Mr. Bounty an offer—nor Soames, nor my bailiff or head groom. I decided to put a notice in the journals instead: 'Desperate widow seeks husband, preferably under ninety years. Must have four limbs, some hair, and a few teeth.

26

Direct inquiries to Whitehern, Sussex.' You will see it in tomorrow's *Morning Observer*."

Nick's lips moved unsteadily. "I take your point," he said, "but I feel you do Bounty an injustice to include him among the octogenarians."

"Do you feel you do my discrimination justice to imply I would offer for a gentleman who is fifty if he's a day and has a daughter older than I am?"

Hansard seldom blushed, but he did feel a little heat about the ears. "I feared the circumstance of your aunt Hildegarde's imminent visit might have pitched you into unusual behavior."

"It did," she said, and met his gaze coolly. "After your categorical refusal, I am not likely to repeat my error."

"I apologize for last night. I was a little surprised—"

"No, Nick, you were gasping in shock, like my old mare Belle with the heaves." Emma realized that this unbuttoned conversation was displeasing Nick and added politely, "I want to thank you for rescuing me from making a wretched mistake by refusing me last night. I realize we would not have suited in the least. I have decided that I shan't marry until I meet some gentleman I can esteem—as you gentlemen say, since you are afraid of the word *love*. Meanwhile, I can look after myself."

"You have braced yourself for Hildegarde's visit, then?" he asked lightly. This had always seemed an excuse to him.

"Miss Foxworth has a cold. Aunt Hildegarde is a practicing hypochondriac. She won't come when there is illness in the house. Miss Foxworth will be in no rush to recover, I promise you."

"Very sly, Emma."

"I have the disadvantage of being a lady. We must use our wits to save ourselves as custom and the law

27

give all the authority to the gentlemen. Had you proposed to me, it would have been considered right and proper. And by the way, about last night . . ."

"Let us agree it didn't happen," he said dismissingly.

"We can't sweep an elephant under the carpet. It happened, and there is just one other thing I ought to have explained last night, only I was so nervous when you pokered up like an outraged spinster that it slipped my mind. I quite forgot about Mrs. Pettigrew. Naturally I did not mean you would have to break with her, for, of course, I meant only a marriage of convenience."

"Very flattering. I understood you meant possibly no marriage at all. If I recall aright, there was some talk of your jilting me."

"Yes. Perhaps you would have gone along with my scheme if you had known my true intention?" she asked daringly.

"That would certainly have made it more palatable," he replied, and watched as her jaw squared in anger. "But then I have my own reputation to consider as well. Folks would be bound to wonder why you broke it off. I would be castigated as either a monster of depravity or some other sort of scoundrel."

"Or Lady Capehart would be called a jilt, no better than she should be," she pointed out.

"That is another possibility. And speaking of ladies' reputations, I must mention that you are slandering an unexceptionable lady to imply Mrs. Pettigrew is my mistress."

"Indeed! It is news to me that unexceptionable ladies send their gentlemen callers home at three o'clock in the morning. I saw you riding down the road at that hour the night before you went to London."

"What were you doing up at three o'clock?"

"Watching you come home from Mrs. Pettigrew's. And looking at the moon," she added with a wistful expression. "It was a full moon. The park looked silver and black. It was beautiful."

Nicholas found himself gazing at Emma. She had a faraway, romantic look in her eyes. He shook himself to attention and said, "As you are interested in what I was doing, I'll tell you: I was attending the foaling of Bounty's broodmare. If the foal was a filly, he was to sell her to me. It was a colt."

"Odd Bounty didn't mention it."

"Odder that you should," he retorted. "There are some things ladies do not discuss with gentlemen, Emma."

She gave a demure smile. "So you told me, last night."

"And you have decided to ignore the lesson?"

"I have decided to set my own boundaries, especially when I am with friends. We are still friends, are we not?" she asked archly.

"Thus far."

"Good," she said, and picked up her book.

Nicholas took it as a hint that she wished to resume her reading. He glanced at the title and was surprised that it was not a gothic novel, but a tome on Grecian antiquities.

"I didn't know you were interested in Greece," he said.

"There is a good deal you don't know about me, Nick. It occurs to me that in the several years we have been acquainted, we've never talked about anything serious—except estate matters, since John's death, of course. I wonder why that is."

Nick cocked his head and grinned. "Perhaps it's because you're young and pretty."

"Or perhaps it's because you're a gazetted flirt. I don't know why young gentlemen think ladies' heads must be gray before their owners are allowed to enjoy sensible conversation. I've often discussed Greece with Bounty. He's quite an expert. Did you know they had slaves?"

Nick felt a sting of annoyance at the recurrence of Bounty's name. "So I've heard."

"It is shocking that everyone puffs Greece up as such a fine model of society. The ladies were treated abominably." She slanted a long, enigmatic look at him. "Even worse than we are treated in England."

"You're sitting at ease in your own garden, which the law allows you to own outright. You control your own estate, your finances. I cannot think you are too hard done by in England."

She gazed off into the trees. "Yes, but everyone still treats me as a child. I know Papa will send Aunt Hildegarde sooner or later. I haven't the freedom of a married lady, yet if I marry, my husband will expect to bearlead me."

With a thought to Lord James, Nicholas said, "What you ought to do is find a biddable husband. You will satisfy the proprieties and still keep the upper hand at home."

"That is exactly what I have been thinking myself. But where is this pineapple of perfection, a biddable husband, to be found?"

"You never know, Emma. He may show up sooner than you think."

"No, I won't find him here. No point fishing for a trout in a rain barrel. Such gentlemen are only to be found in London." She said the last word reverently, as if it were sacred.

"I caught an excellent trout in my own river," he said, smiling.

"I was speaking metaphorically, Nick."

He took his leave in good spirits. James would not be a severe husband. He was an easygoing fellow, good natured and handsome. Perhaps a little too easygoing for a girl in Emma's frame of mind? He shook the wisp of doubt away. The situation was too volatile to leave as it was. Most certainly Emma would marry someone very soon, and it was best to make sure that someone was a proper gentleman.

Chapter Five

Emma assumed it was one of those coincidences, whose long arms are so famous, that brought Derek Hunter to Whitehern the next afternoon. Miss Foxworth had been putting her nephew forward as a *parti* ever since John's death. And now, just when it was possible for Emma to be thinking of marrying, he appeared in the flesh. In fact, Miss Foxworth had had more to do with it than had coincidence. She regularly dispatched notes to her favorite nephew. In the last she had said that Lady Capehart was now putting off her crape and going into Society again.

Derek Hunter waited only long enough to have his hair trimmed and to lay his watch on the pawnbroker's shelf to pay for his new jacket before setting off for a visit. The tailor refused to part with the vestment without some payment for past services. Hunter made an unfashionable and inconvenient arrival mere moments before dinner. As it was only his aunt and Emma who were there, it was no matter. Miss Foxworth was sufficiently recovered from her sniffles to come down to dinner. Emma was curious to see this Adonis of whom she had heard so much. So far as appearance went, she was not disappointed.

He was tall and well built, with a glistening head of hair so blond it was nearly white. A pair of sapphire blue eyes of startling clarity peeped out from his tanned, healthy face. His jacket, while not the work of Weston—it was by Stutz—showed his shoulders off to perfect advantage. He was accoutred with all the trinkets of the dandy. A quizzing glass hung on a black, corded ribbon. A gold watch fob, attached to a thick gold chain, dangled from his pocket. The watch that went with it was on the shelf in London, but the fob and chain looked well. His pockets held an assortment of items: snuffbox, dice, cards (both playing and calling), and a spent bullet that had been prized out of his shinbone after he was shot by a highwayman with exceedingly poor aim.

He lifted the quizzing glass when Miss Foxworth presented him to Lady Capehart and studied her for a moment through it, before speaking in a practiced drawl.

"By Jove!" he exclaimed. "How does it come London hasn't heard of you, Lady Capehart?"

"I cannot imagine," she replied, "for I have certainly heard of London."

"A wit!" he exclaimed. "It is unusual to find beauty and intelligence in one lady." And wealth into the bargain, he added to himself. He opened his lips to reveal a set of perfect pearls, marred by having the corners filed down to allow him to whistle like a mail-coach driver during a dry spell in which he had thoroughly enjoyed that occupation.

"You make your home in London, I believe, Mr. Hunter?" Emma said.

"I keep a set of rooms there—a pied-à-terre for the Season, you know. One must do the pretty with the debs, or the mamas fly into the boughs, but I spend most of my time in the country."

"Emma is very eager to spend some time in London, Derek," Miss Foxworth prompted.

"I should say so! There's nowhere like it. As old

33

Johnson was saying t'other day, when a man is tired of London, he is tired of life."

Emma frowned. She recognized the quotation and knew perfectly well Dr. Johnson had been buried in the last century. But perhaps Mr. Hunter meant some other Johnson who had quoted the doctor. It was a common name after all.

Mr. Hunter continued to outline the delights of London. "Drury Lane, Covent Garden, the balls, routs, ridottos—and Vauxhall, of course! You really must allow me to take you ladies up to London for a few days."

Emma listened, enthralled. Those were exactly the things she longed to see and do. Now that she was out of mourning, she also had shopping to do to update her wardrobe. And it would be lovely to have an escort for the evening.

"What a charming idea!" she exclaimed.

"Pity I didn't bring my traveling carriage," he said. "I decided to drive my curricle as the weather was so fine."

"Emma has a carriage," Miss Foxworth said.

"I'm sorry I sold my London house, or I could put you up there," was Mr. Hunter's next misleading statement. "It was too large for a bachelor. A great barn of a place on Grosvenor Square, next door to Lord Harrington. I took a set of rooms instead."

These artful speeches made Emma think he was very well to grass. Miss Foxworth had been vague on that point, but his style of life certainly indicated wealth.

"I rather enjoy staying at hotels," she said.

Before long Soames announced dinner.

"And here I sit in my buckskins!" Mr. Hunter exclaimed. "You will think me no better than I should be, Lady Capehart, but I shan't make you sit down to cold mutton on my account. Just close your eyes, and pretend I am properly outfitted. I ought to have brought my valet with me, but he dislikes the open carriage. I am too soft by half with my servants." Of course he had no valet.

"That's quite all right, Mr. Hunter," Emma said. "It is only ourselves. Sir John's valet is still with us. He will look after you for the nonce."

"And after dinner we shall have a friendly game of cards to pass the time, eh?" He was assured of picking up enough blunt to treat the ladies to dinner and a play in London.

"We don't usually play for money, Derek," his aunt warned him.

"Egad, I'm not talking about gambling! Pennies a point—or perhaps a shilling a point, to make it interesting." Miss Foxworth gasped. "Not much point shuffling pieces of paper about if there is no sport of winning a little something in it," he said, smiling. "I'm sure a nabob like Lady Capehart has no objection to a shilling a point."

Every word that left his lips raised him higher in her regard. She didn't want to look like a Johnnie Raw and agreed that a shilling a point would make the game interesting.

He kept the ladies well amused during dinner, with apocryphal tales of house parties he had attended at sundry noble homes, balls, hunts in which he had led the field, races won, and other dashing doings that showed him to advantage. During the course of his stories, he put himself in Scotland shooting one morning and hunting at Badminton that same afternoon, but as Emma had no idea that Badminton was in the Cotswold hills, she didn't find it strange.

35

It was the naive Miss Foxworth who said, "Is Badminton in Scotland, Derek?"

"Did I say Badminton? I meant Badderhurst, old Lord MacIntosh's place, in Scotland."

"Badderhurst doesn't sound Scottish," Miss Foxworth said.

Hunter glared her into silence. "No, it don't, but it is. By Jove, this is excellent mutton, Lady Capehart."

Mr. Hunter consumed a hearty dinner, praising every bite that entered his mouth. When it was done, he wafted his hand as if he were the host and told the ladies he would join them in the saloon as soon as he had gargled a glass of port.

"What do you think of him, Emma?" Miss Foxworth asked eagerly.

"He's very handsome."

"And so lively. Very amusing, is he not?"

"Vastly amusing."

"Derek knows everyone. He will show us a good time in London."

When he joined them a little later, Miss Foxworth said, "Perhaps you could take Emma to a ball, Derek, if any of your friends happen to be having one while we are there."

"By Jove! Wouldn't the fine lords stare to see her!" he exclaimed, with a long, approving look at Emma. "Of course you were presented at court, Lady Capehart?"

"No, I wasn't," she said apologetically.

"Pity, but Society is fierce in that respect. No presentation, no balls." He took a pinch of snuff and sneezed daintily into his handkerchief.

"Perhaps a small, private party," Miss Foxworth suggested.

"Unfortunately, with the Season as close to over as

makes no difference, the lords have all run off to their estates, or Brighton."

"Perhaps we should go to Brighton," Miss Foxworth said.

Mr. Hunter gave a chiding look. "It is London that Lady Capehart has set her heart on, Auntie. I hope I can show you a good time without noble balls. And now, shall we set up the card table?"

Mr. Hunter managed to relieve his hostess of five pounds, which he deemed enough for the trip. It took him a few hours to do it, for he disliked to risk using shaved cards, and his hostess proved a daunting player.

"Beginner's luck! I shan't insult you by not taking the money, Lady Capehart," he said, scooping up the gold and sliding it into his pocket. "Tomorrow evening when you fleece me, I shall insist that you keep your winnings."

"I shall hold you to that, sir," she replied.

It was late, and after Soames brought them a light snack, they retired. The next morning Mr. Hunter expressed his regret that he hadn't brought his hack with him, for he craved some exercise. Emma immediately offered him the loan of Sir John's mount. He rode about Emma's estate, mentally adding up the value of the acres, farms, and herd, and wondering if the sale of the cattle would bring enough cash to buy a couple of thoroughbreds. The chit was a nabob, by gad! As green as grass and as pretty as could stare. Dame Fortune had smiled on him at last.

Lord Hansard was perturbed the next morning when he spotted the dashing young buck from his stable. He made an excuse that afternoon to call on Emma to discover who he was.

He found Emma alone, writing a fictitious report to her papa on the progress of Miss Foxworth's indisposition. Mr. Hunter had darted into the village in his curricle to see what further amusement the place offered to the future master of Whitehern. Miss Foxworth was resting abovestairs, to rally her strength for the trip to London.

Soames called Lady Capehart from the study when Hansard arrived. She found him in the saloon, frowning at the quizzing glass that Derek had left on the table. He lifted the glass and said, "A visitor, Emma?"

"Yes, Miss Foxworth's nephew is paying us a visit."

"Hunter?"

"Yes, Derek Hunter."

"Long threatening comes at last. John often mentioned Hunter. You won't want to encourage the likes of him."

"I didn't realize you had Mr. Hunter's acquaintance," she said coolly.

"I haven't."

"Yet you feel qualified to tell me I shouldn't encourage him. He is vastly handsome and amusing."

"Your late husband often spoke of him. As John isn't here to look out for your interests, I shall risk incurring your wrath by saying bluntly, the fellow is on the prowl for an heiress. He is here in an effort to capture your fortune."

"But that's ridiculous! He's very well connected. He knows everyone."

"Introductions don't cost anything. A handsome face, a little brass, and ingenuity are all that's required. He's penniless."

"I believe you are mistaken about his finances, but if my fortune is to be captured by someone, then I

38

should prefer it be a gentleman who is at least amusing."

"Don't be ridiculous!" he said angrily. "You know perfectly well it won't do. Good God, he'd squander your estate within the year and have you begging in the streets. It is clear you intend to marry someone, but you don't have to settle for the likes of Hunter. William Bounty would be a better match. Any gentleman would be glad to have you."

"So I am universally appealing to every gentleman except yourself?" she said, with a sharp look. "It happens I do not want another—a country bumpkin sort of husband like William," she said, coloring in embarrassment. John had been a countrified gentleman. "I want a dashing fellow who is at home amid the ton. When I married John he said he would take me to London, but every time I mentioned it, he found some excuse and only bought me another bonnet or piece of jewelry instead." She pouted in memory.

Nicholas had noticed the quantity of clothes and jewelry Emma bought and despised her for it. He realized now that they had been consolation prizes.

"I expect he was afraid to take you to London," he said. "He feared you would set up a flirtation."

Her nostrils pinched in annoyance. "If you mean I would be unfaithful to my husband, pray have the courage of your convictions and say so. I always flirted with you. He didn't mind that. And don't you dare say I would ever be unfaithful!"

"I didn't say you would. I said John probably feared it. He was a deal older than you, after all. About London, Emma, I think you overestimate its pleasures."

"I notice you never miss a Season!"

39

"True, but like most gentlemen, I spend the greater part of the year on my estate."

"Well, I want someone who would be at home in either place, like you. I don't mean you!" she added hastily.

"I have fallen in your esteem since the other evening, then?" he asked mischievously.

"Don't crow so loud, milord. You'll lay an egg. Nothing makes a gentleman so unattractive to a lady as making her look a perfect fool by refusing her offer—unless it is constantly throwing it in her face. I thought we were to forget it."

"I wonder if I wasn't overhasty in my refusal," he said playfully. "Perhaps I was only playing hard to get."

"If that was the case, then you made a grave error in judgment. And I hardly think you would do that— where ladies are concerned. But it is kind of you to try to assuage my wounded pride."

"And not your broken heart?"

"Oh, my heart is not so fragile as all that."

"Well, I would like to do more than assuage your wounded pride, Emma," he said.

She looked at him with a startled question in her eyes. Good God! Was he going to accept after all?

Nicholas had some inkling of her thoughts and spoke on hastily to prevent any more misunderstandings. "You mentioned the lack of a father or guardian to oversee your match."

Emma's racing heart slowed to a thud. "I'm not sure I want a match at this time," she said.

"You soon will. I am offering my services to vet the candidates."

She considered this a moment. It would certainly separate the wheat from the chaff to have Nicholas look them over. If Derek Hunter was really a fortune hunter, he had most assuredly taken her in with his fine talk of all his noble friends.

"You want to insure I marry someone who will make you a good neighbor, in other words," she said, undeceived by his offer of assistance.

"And you a good husband," he said. "Our interests are not mutually exclusive. They overlap on this point. We both want a good manager running Whitehern."

"Actually, it's not a bad idea, since I am a regular greenhead," she said reluctantly. "Very well, you can begin by having a chat with Mr. Hunter."

As that was exactly what Nicholas had in mind, he agreed. He would send a note, asking Hunter to join him for a ride the next morning.

When Mr. Hunter raised the stakes to two shillings a point and relieved Emma of seven pounds that evening at cards, she began to suspect he was no better than he should be. She remembered his having said he had spoken to Dr. Johnson, and that he had been shooting in Scotland in the morning and hunting at Badminton in the afternoon. He only wanted to drop a noble name into the conversation.

She noticed, too, that the delights of London that Mr. Hunter spoke of were all open to the public. He had balked at attending any private parties. Plays and Vauxhall Gardens required only the price of admission. Perhaps it *was* a good idea to have Nick look over her potential suitors.

Chapter Six

When Soames handed Hunter a note that evening, Hunter took it nervously, expecting a dun at best and at worst a challenge due to a certain card game last week. He fanned his fingers in such a way that no bystander could get a glance at the note. It would be difficult to say whether he was more astonished or flattered to read that Lord Hansard would be pleased if Mr. Hunter would do him the honor of riding with him the next morning.

It took him a moment to compose his voice into its usual bored drawl to relay the message to the ladies.

"Lord Hansard wants me to ride out with him tomorrow," he said. "Decent of him. Can't say I remember meeting the fellow. Must have been at one of my clubs—Brooke's, very likely." Mr. Hunter was familiar with the facade of Brooke's and knew it was the sort of club where gentlemen like Lord Hansard might be met, if only a fellow were allowed in.

"I expect it's a compliment to Emma," Miss Foxworth explained. "Lord Hansard is a bosom bow of Emma's."

"The pity of it is, my mount hasn't arrived. I asked my man to send it on. A dashed fine Arabian gelding."

"You must use John's mount again," Emma said at once.

At least Hunter had no concern for his riding skills. He was a bruising rider, and with Sir John's handsome mount beneath him, he made a suitable-looking partner for Hansard when they rode out the next morning.

One glance at him was enough for Nick to see why Emma had succumbed to the fellow's charms. Hunter didn't try his name-dropping stunts with a nobleman who would actually know the people concerned. The talk was of boxing matches and horse races, until Hansard redirected it to crops and herds and farming matters, at which time Nick did most of the talking. Hunter listened and learned.

"What would a spread like Whitehern be worth?" he asked, in a nonchalant voice.

"Around thirty thousand," Nick replied.

Hunter swallowed his delight and ran his eyes over the lush acres. "Plenty of land to raise a few horses as well," he said.

"Are you interested in horse breeding?" Nick asked.

"Race horses are my weakness."

E'er long Nick was being inundated with a tide of ill-informed horse-breeding lore. He found Hunter amusing company—and the worst possible match for Emma. It was clear as a pikestaff that what Hunter had in mind was to sell off the herd of cattle and turn Whitehern into a horse-breeding farm.

After riding for nearly two hours, they stopped at Waterdown for a glass of ale and exchanged a friendly farewell, before Hunter returned to White-hern for lunch.

"Did you have a nice ride, Derek?" Miss Foxworth asked.

"An excellent ride. Hansard's a decent chap. I liked him."

43

Emma was glad Nick hadn't said or done anything to offend her guest. She was also extremely curious to hear Nick's account of the ride. But before this occurred, Hunter took her for a spin in his curricle that afternoon. He was an accomplished fiddler, but the sort who had to pass every rig on the road. It was a matter of pride that he set a pace of sixteen miles an hour, no matter how bumpy the road, how much dust he raised, or how often his passenger begged him to slow down.

"You call this fast?" he laughed, and whipped up the team to an even more reckless speed.

No conversation was possible at such a pace. When they alighted in the village, all windblown and breathless, to stroll along the High Street, Mr. Hunter evinced no interest in ancient architecture or the pretty little church. His two subjects of conversation were horse breeding and horse races. It was as if water had been building up behind a dam those few days he had spent in being civil, and now it all came gushing out to inundate her. Mr. Hunter had caught a whiff of accomplishing his life's dream, and he could no more stop talking than he could stop breathing. His bored drawl gave way to excited chatter.

"That's very expensive though, is it not?" Emma asked.

"Aye, it is, but there's money in it. Spend a sprat to catch a mackerel. You could start in a small way right at Whitehern. That west pasture would make a dandy training track. It's already as close to being flat as makes no difference."

He went on to outline how this might be done, by smoothing it out, covering the lush pasture in sand, building fences, and such things. It seemed a special barn would also be required. "You could fell the trees from your own forest. It wouldn't cost a sou, but for the bit of labor. Your tenant farmers could throw the barn up for you."

"Very interesting, but I know nothing about horse racing," she said.

He slid a winsome smile in her direction. "Of course, you'd have to have a fellow who knew what he was doing to help you," he said, and was soon ranting about joining the Jockey Club and winning races at Ascot. Before they reached home Emma knew precisely what was in Hunter's mind. He hadn't stopped in front of the jewelry shop and gazed at the engagement rings for no reason. It was her estate that was to be turned into another Chevely Park, and her money that was to finance the race horses.

Mr. Hunter couldn't settle down to playing cards with the ladies that evening. He was too excited. When he suggested taking a spin into the village after dinner, Emma didn't try to stop him.

"A chap I know will be stopping at the inn on his way to his estate," he lied. "We'll have a few wets. I shan't be late, but don't wait up for me."

"Don't rush yourself," Emma said, very politely. "I'm sure you must find it dull, here in the country."

For herself, she found the peace and quiet welcome after so many hours of Mr. Hunter's incessant chatter. She felt, as well, that Nick might come that evening to report on his ride with her guest. Shortly before nine the door knocker sounded, and Soames announced, "Lord Hansard."

Lord Hansard stepped into the saloon. His understated elegance showed to even better advantage than usual, with the memory of Mr. Hunter's gaudy paste ruby and extravagant cravat still in Emma's mind. Hansard peered around to see if Hunter was there, then entered to make his bows to the ladies. His voice had the calming effect of a mild zephyr after the tumultuous raptures of Mr. Hunter on the glories of race horses.

After a few moments of general conversation, Nick directed a questioning look at Emma. She rose and said, "Nick has come to help me with some estate matters, Miss Foxworth. We'll go into the study, so we shan't disturb you."

Miss Foxworth smiled and picked up her novel.

"Well, what is your verdict?" Emma asked when they were seated on the bergère chairs by the grate, with a glass of wine at their elbows.

"I liked him," Nick said.

Emma's gray eyes opened wider. "Really!"

"As a person, he's good-natured and entertaining—and, of course, handsome." He looked at her appraisingly.

"That would be of interest to you, of course!"

"Only in so much as it would concern you. He would do well enough for the lower strata of London Society, but I doubt he would make a satisfactory country husband for the rest of the year." He watched her closely to see her reaction. Emma displayed no disappointment at his verdict.

"He's bored with us already. He went into the village to meet a friend, or so he said."

"I wondered where he was. But actually I was speaking of his husbandry, not his making you a satisfactory husband in a social sense. If I read him aright, his intention is to root out the herd and raise race horses."

"Heresy indeed to a cow lover like yourself. Every horse is to be a Derby winner, though! You must own that would be exciting."

He looked at her in alarm, until he saw the

laughter lurking in her dark eyes. "I see he has discussed his plans with you."

"Certainly he has, ad nauseam. He thinks I would show them all the way in a box at Ascot. He was wondering if you would sponsor him into the Jockey Club. I don't even want to know what *that* would cost me."

"May I assume, then, that you will refuse the offer he is planning to make—and in the not-too-distant future, if I am any judge of a man's intentions?"

"Of course I shan't marry him, but I hope he doesn't offer until after our trip to London. I'm looking forward to that."

Nicholas felt a stab of annoyance, followed by an urge to offer to take Emma and Miss Foxworth to London himself. Except that he had invited Cousin James for that visit, and he could hardly be away when he arrived.

"What would your papa say if he discovered you had gone jaunting off to London?" he asked.

"I can't think he would find out, but if he asked, I could say I took Miss Foxworth to visit a special doctor."

"Lying to your papa?" he chided.

"I could ask her to visit a doctor. Only if Papa asks. I'm sure he won't. I had a note from him today. He says Aunt Hildegarde has had the cold that's going around, so she doesn't fear catching Miss Foxworth's dose. In fact, Hildegarde is in unusual good health and can come to me at any time. I shall have to invent a monsoon in the neighborhood. So horrid for a chronic invalid—all that water."

"I am disappointed in you, Emma," he said sternly.

She made a childish pout and said, "You don't know Hildegarde."

"I know the type. She will have subscribed to the local journals to see if your name is in them, and to discover potential husbands for you. You'll never get away with a monsoon. That would be national news. You must make it a domestic disaster, something that wouldn't be reported in the local journals."

"You are a complete hand, Nick! Here I thought you were going to read me a scold."

"This is a scold. I dislike to see incompetent lying. If a thing is worth doing, it's worth doing right."

"Very edifying advice for you to be giving a young widow," she teased, with a smile that brought out the dimples at the corners of her lips. "What do you, as an accomplished liar, recommend to a tyro like myself?"

He accepted this ambiguous speech in good grace. "A leaking roof, ill-fitting windows that are being replaced. Either of those could see you through the better part of the summer. And who knows, by then you might very well have found your biddable, versatile husband, who is at home in either city or country."

"I don't see how I shall meet him if I don't get to London, and for longer than a few days. I know all the local gentlemen. There isn't a good match in the lot of them." Nick lifted an eyebrow in mock dismay. She patted his knee and gave an easy smile. "Present company is always excepted, Nick. You have already refused me. You had your chance—you shan't have another."

"Bite your tongue, Lady Capehart! Not from you, perhaps. I take leave to tell you, you're not the only fish in the sea. I am expecting an offer from the Dowager Countess of Reeves any day now. Why else has she asked me to sell her carriage and team for her? She plans to plunk her ancient bones in my rig.

48

It is an obvious ploy. She'll get me into her study, ply me with brandy, and press an offer of marriage on me."

"And here you tried to tell me it was not the thing for a lady to offer! Why, the dowager is top of the trees. Her son is in the cabinet."

"That's her grandson. Her son is only a lowly back bencher."

He was glad to see they could laugh about Emma's proposal. It seemed to have brought them closer together.

"I had a letter from my cousin Lord James Philmore this morning," he said a moment later. "He'll be stopping at Waterdown for a few weeks. I'll have a party for him, perhaps a rout party."

She gave him a knowing look. "How convenient. Lord James—that would be a younger son?"

"Yes, his papa is Lord Revson, an eminent Tory."

"And has Lord James an estate of his own?"

"No," he admitted, "but some expectations from an uncle."

"Another penniless gentleman in other words."

"No, a penniless nobleman."

"I am not a title chaser, Nick."

"It confers a few social advantages," he said. "I can assure you James is equally at home in either town or country. He spends every Season in London at his papa's mansion on Berkeley Square. Naturally his wife would do the same. James is tip of the ton."

Emma listened, her interest rising. "Biddable?" she asked.

"Within reason, I believe. You wouldn't want a mere pup."

"What does he look like?" she asked.

"I would say rather handsome, except that he is

said to resemble myself. Picture him looking like me, only younger and handsome."

Emma examined her guest, trying to imagine him younger and more handsome. "When is he coming?"

"You were supposed to say I am handsome, Emma! Really, you must work on your flirting skills if you mean to tackle London."

"Oh, pardon me. You are handsome, Lord Hansard," she said perfunctorily. "When is Lord James coming?"

"In a few days' time." He scowled playfully. "It would help if you could put a little enthusiasm into your niggardly compliments. I shall be introducing James to the local Society at the party. Wear your prettiest frock. The competition will be fierce."

"I thought you said he resembled you?"

Nick took a deep breath. "Lo, how the mighty have fallen," he murmured. "Proposals one evening, insults the next."

"We have agreed to forget that proposal!"

"I do try, but I find it keeps coming back—" Emma looked at him with interest. "Like a toothache," he added.

"Try oil of cloves. I hope you don't have the party while I'm in London!"

"Why do you not put off the trip until after the party?"

"We haven't set a definite time." Emma was less eager for the trip since she had learned Derek was so shabby. "Very well, we shall wait until after your rout. It will be my first party since John's death. I shall feel nervous as a deb."

He lifted his glass and examined Emma over the rim. "Don't worry. You'll be the prettiest lady there." She gave him a little smile, then he added blandly, "I shan't invite the Lawry girls, or Miss Blenkinsop, or—"

"Or the Dowager Countess of Reeves."

"Oh, I must invite her. Isn't it nice that you've found someone other than William Bounty with whom you can have some intelligent conversation, Emma?" he asked facetiously. "We were not used to being so intellectual in our little tête-à-têtes."

"Very true. You were used to flirt with me, when I was safely married to John. Well, it is my own fault, after all, for frightening you. And now we must return to the saloon. We cannot leave Miss Foxworth alone all evening."

He put on a face of mock alarm. "Do you think it's safe?"

"What do you mean?"

"I'm pretty sure she has her eye on me as well. Don't leave me alone with her."

"That offer went to your head, Nick. One would think you had never been courted before."

He rose and lifted her fingers to his lips. "Never by such an Incomparable—until I met the Dowager Countess, of course."

She wrenched her hand free and strode out the door, hiding her smile behind stiff shoulders.

Chapter Seven

Derek Hunter had still not returned when Emma retired at midnight. His bleary eyes, when he came to the breakfast parlor the next morning, suggested he had been out late and drinking hard. Immediately after breakfast he asked Emma out to ride, mentioning that his Arabian gelding should be here by now. As this imaginary horse had not appeared, he rode the late Sir John's mount. As they cantered through her meadows and pastures, he pressed on her the changes that would be required to turn Whitehern into a stud farm.

"I'm really not at all interested in that, Mr. Hunter," she said firmly.

When they stopped by the pond to rest, Mr. Hunter showed her to a grassy surface and dropped down beside her. He removed his curled beaver and gazed out over her land with a proprietary eye. He saw not a rich, thriving dairy farm, with a new crop of calves insuring future prosperity, but a stud farm manqué. The location, too, was excellent. There wasn't a good stud farm in this southeastern corner of England.

Emma admired him, as he admired her estate. His platinum hair and blue eyes had never looked more delightful. He turned and saw her gazing at him. It was all the encouragement he required. Before she could stop him, he had seized her hand and began pressing compliments on her.

"So beautiful, so unspoiled."

She wrenched her hand away. "Really, Mr. Hunter! You mustn't say such things."

"Let me speak my heart, Emma. You're just the sort of game chick I always hoped to find. I think you and I would deal very well. You know all about me from Aunt Miriam. It's not as though we're strangers after all. I wouldn't have spoken so soon, but it happens I met a fellow last night who has an excellent Arab stud up for sale. He's only asking a thousand pounds for him."

"A thousand pounds!"

"Incredible, isn't it? He's worth two or three times that. It happens that I'm a little short at the moment, just until next quarter day. I wouldn't borrow from you unless there was an understanding between us." He recaptured her fingers and squeezed them in a paralyzing grip, while his sapphire orbs gleamed into hers. "You know what I mean. Naturally I'll repay you every sou."

"No, really, Mr. Hunter, I am not at all interested." She managed to free her fingers. They ached from his grip.

"Dash it, where's your imagination, Emma? It's the chance of a lifetime."

"The chance of your lifetime, perhaps. Not mine. I must tell you, Mr. Hunter, I have no intention of marrying a man I met only three days ago, nor of turning a very profitable dairy farm into a place to lose money breeding horses. I hope I have not misled you into thinking I am interested in anything of the sort."

"But Aunt Miriam said—"

"Your aunt reads a good deal of romantic fiction," Emma said firmly, and rose to brush off her skirts.

He drew himself slowly to his feet, gazed once more over the estate, and uttered a deep, heartfelt sigh.

Emma felt Mr. Hunter would be leaving that same day. It meant losing out on the trip to London, but after his proposal, the trip could not be anything but embarrassing. He would either be in a huff or take advantage of the enforced proximity to press his offer forward again. She hardly knew which would be worse.

Mr. Hunter took a more optimistic view of matters. He knew he had lost out on Emma's fortune and his dream of a stud farm, but that didn't mean he couldn't pass a few weeks in the lap of luxury at Whitehern without expense. He mentally abandoned the trip to London. It was bound to cost him money—have to entertain the ladies a little. And besides, there were people there who would be dunning him for unpaid bills.

"You have spoken. We'll say no more about it. Still, no reason we can't be friends," he said, his good humor unimpaired. "Aunt Miriam mentioned Hansard is having a little do. He would be offended if I darted off before it takes place."

Emma had told Miss Foxworth of the party. Miss Foxworth had apparently told her nephew, but why he should think Nick would be offended if he didn't come was a mystery.

"Suit yourself," Emma replied. "I'm sure Miss Foxworth's nephew is always welcome at Whitehern."

His pearly teeth flashed in the sunlight. "That's dashed decent of you, Emma."

It was another proposal that seemed to bring Emma closer to the other participant. Hunter and Emma were soon on a first-name basis. Now that he didn't have to keep up a facade, he relaxed and enjoyed himself. When he wasn't riding John's horse—the tale of the Arabian gelding was heard no more—he was flying about the countryside in his curricle. In the evenings he usually went into the village to spend a few hours drinking and playing cards with new friends at the local tavern. He always made friends quickly. He even visited Lord Hansard a few times, storing up anecdotes to impress his acquaintances when he returned to London.

Nick called on Emma the evening after Mr. Hunter's proposal to give her the invitations to his rout party. Hunter was out, but Emma was glad to see there was an invitation for him as well. She felt sorry for Hunter's hand-to-mouth existence, but as he enjoyed himself so much, she didn't have to feel too sorry. Miss Foxworth was in the saloon. If she had heard of her nephew's setback, she kept it to herself. She sat with her nose in a book as usual, paying no attention to the caller after greeting him.

"I'll bring young James over to meet you the afternoon before the rout, to give you the inside track," Nick said, as he handed Emma the invitations.

"You feel I have to be handicapped, do you?"

"Spoken like a racetrack tout, Lady Capehart. I see Hunter has been at you with his schemes. Have you succumbed to the blandishment of Ascot?"

"Certainly not. I refused his offer."

"He's already offered!"

"Well, I think marriage was included in his offer to run my stud farm for me," she replied.

"No grass growing under Mr. Hunter's boots! One would think an experienced rider would know better than to rush his fences. Has he left Whitehern, then?"

"Oh, no. He will be happy to attend your soiree. I

55

seem to get along well with all the partners in my proposals, whether rejecter or rejectee. Which reminds me, how is the Dowager Countess of Reeves doing, Nick?"

He shook his head sadly. "I didn't get my offer after all. She found someone else to sell her carriage and team for her, after leading me on shamelessly, the wanton hussy."

"There is still Miss Foxworth," Emma said supportively.

Miss Foxworth looked up at the mention of her name. "What's that you say, Emma?"

Emma gave a guilty start. It was Lord Hansard who replied. "Emma was just saying you will be attending my little rout party," he said.

"Oh, indeed, I shall. Derek is looking forward to it." Her social duty done, she smiled and returned her attention to the perils of her heroine.

"You haven't been practicing your lying technique, Lady Capehart," Nick said severely. "You were shaken by your chaperon's question."

"Not been practicing? You should have seen the letter I wrote to Papa this very day. My roof is in a shocking state. Not only the lead surface but the subfloor must be replaced. The roofer says it will take a couple of months—and a deal of banging and mess."

"You're coming along," he complimented. "Written lies are only the first step, however. Your first-class liar can look his companion in the eye and tell a whisker without blushing."

"Then there is no point pestering you for further details of that cousin you are trying to palm off on me. I doubt Lord James has any expectations at all. He is probably ugly as sin into the bargain."

"No, he doesn't really look that much like me."

"Oh, but you're handsome as can stare, Nick!" A surprised smile alit on his swarthy features. "Am I improving?" she asked archly. "Yes, I think you actually swallowed that plumper," she said, and enjoyed a good laugh at his expense.

"I shall be taking lessons from you in no time. It never pays to teach a fish to swim."

"Are you saying that ladies are natural-born liars?"

"I would never be so foolhardy as to tell a lady the truth. I only infer that they have an uncommon aptitude for prevarication. And now let us talk sense. What is the status of the trip to London with Hunter?"

"We haven't mentioned it since the proposal. I rather think it's off, unfortunately."

Nick swallowed his relief and said, "Ah, pity. Perhaps we can set something up with James."

"Let us see how he and I rub along first. Your notion and mine of what constitutes a handsome, conversable gentleman may be at odds."

Before he could reply there was a knock at the door. William Bounty had chosen that evening to drop in on Emma. That he was wearing his best evening jacket and carrying a big bouquet of roses from his garden suggested that it was a courting visit. He looked disappointed to find Lord Hansard there.

"How lovely!" Emma said, accepting the bouquet. Soames took it away to put the roses in water.

Behind Bounty's back Nick gave a cynical grin.

Emma invited Bounty to have a seat.

He sat and said, "I am off to London tomorrow, Lady Capehart. I just stopped to ask if there is any commission I can perform for you. No trouble, I assure you. Indeed, it would be a pleasure."

"That's very kind of you, Mr. Bounty," Emma

replied, "but I can't think of anything I need at the moment."

Bounty had received his invitation to Nick's rout, and they spoke of that for a moment. Emma inquired for his daughter and granddaughters. When Emma offered him a glass of wine, he declined and took his leave. It was clear to Bounty that Hansard planned to make a night of it. No courting could occur under his cynical gaze.

After he had left, Nick said, "There is another potential London guide for you, Emma. Bounty goes often to London to check up on the East India Company. He has some shares in John's Company."

"Oh, I hardly think Mr. Bounty would be interested in the theater or such depravities. His notion of a big night is to attend a concert of antique music." She smiled fondly at the roses when Soames brought them in. "He is very sweet and thoughtful, of course," she added pensively.

Nick felt a little shiver of apprehension. Her recent run-in with Hunter might have given her a taste for a good, solid, respectable gent like Bounty. He was not that different in either age or interests from John, and she had seemed happy enough with him.

"At his age he wouldn't want to be attending plays," he said firmly. "James is interested in the theater," he added, for no other reason than to put his nephew forward.

Emma gave him a knowing smile. "I shall wait until I have met this penniless paragon before falling in love with him. I have learned from experience that gentlemen are not always as they are described by their relatives. Miss Foxworth forgot to mention her nephew is penniless. I wonder what you are not telling me about Lord James?"

"If I have told you nothing but his good points, it is because I know no ill of him."

"You cannot be very close to him, though. I never heard you mention him before I threw you into a pelter by revealing my unmaidenly rush to leap at the altar."

"I have known him from the cradle," Nick said.

It wasn't a complete lie. He had known of James forever. He spoke on about his cousin for quite ten minutes, ransacking his mind for any praiseworthy details Lady Revson might have mentioned about her son in her occasional letters.

Emma listened, but was not convinced. "If he's as wonderful as you say, you'd be looking higher than a baronet's widow for him," she said bluntly.

Her plain speaking quite took the wind out of Nick's sails. He suggested a game of cards and stayed for another hour without mentioning Lord James.

When Miss Foxworth began gathering up her wraps to retire, he took his leave of the ladies, promising to bring Lord James to call the next afternoon.

Chapter Eight

Lord Hansard was well impressed with Lord James when his cousin arrived at Waterdown the next day to begin his visit. Nick's greatest fear was that James, at twenty-two, might be a little immature for Emma. Although she was also twenty-two, she had been married for a few years and had the management of Whitehern since John's passing. But when he saw Lord James, his fear vanished.

The lad was as sober and mature as a judge. His conversation was entirely sensible. James related any new occurrences within his family to Nick—a match for his sister Meg was in the offing and his papa had procured another sinecure at court. Next James inquired for any new doings at Waterdown and listened with apparent interest to Nick's answer.

"What of yourself, James?" Nick asked later. "What are your plans?"

"You are referring to that harebrained scheme I had when I was young of buying a cornet and going to the Peninsula to fight the Frenchies. I gave that up some time ago."

"I'm happy to hear it."

"Yes, I feel my calling lies elsewhere. The church," James said somberly.

"Ah." This was less pleasing, but a younger son had to make his own way in the world. No doubt

James would be happy to exchange a meager living for being master of Whitehern.

At Whitehern, Miss Foxworth had mentioned to Derek that Nick was bringing his cousin to call before the rout. Derek, wanting to please Emma, said the next afternoon that he would remain to meet Lord James.

When the expected call was made, Emma looked with interest for her first view of Lord James. Nick was correct—there was a resemblance between the cousins. Lord James was tall and well formed, with dark hair and eyes. He wore his hair cropped close to his head, brushed back, not forward in the more stylish do. His build was slighter than Nick's, and his toilette less elegant. His cravat was simply folded, and the buttons on his jacket were small. But overall he made a good, gentlemanly appearance.

His bow, when he was presented, had a certain simple grace.

"Hansard has told me a good deal about you, Lady Capehart," he said, in a low, velvety voice.

"You mustn't believe everything your cousin says," she replied lightly.

Lord James appeared baffled. "I'm sure Cousin Nick would never trifle with the truth," he said.

Emma couldn't believe the young gentleman Nick had been puffing off to her could be so obtuse. She assumed her guest had the same playful disposition as Nick and retorted, "No indeed, there is nothing trifling in Nick's way of falsifying matters."

"Lady Capehart is jesting, James," Nick said.

"Ah. I'm not sure it's wise to trifle with a gentleman's reputation, Lady Capehart," he said. His gentle voice made it less a reprimand than a suggestion.

Emma looked a question at Nick. He shrugged his

61

shoulders and spoke to Mr. Hunter. Before long the company was laughing at some foolishness having to do with a fixed horse race. Lord James listened closely, shaking his head in dismay. Tea was brought in and the conversation continued. Nick kept Hunter occupied to allow his cousin to make headway with Emma.

"Do you live with your parents at Revson Hall, Lord James?" Emma asked.

"I have been, until the present, except for the Season, of course, when one goes to London. It's time I find my own way in the world. I have pretty well decided to enter the clergy."

"I expect your papa has a good living at his disposal?" she asked. Like Nick, she assumed a younger son would leap at the chance of stepping into an excellent estate instead. James's reply caused a doubt.

"He has two or three, but I have no opinion of plurality. One church and one flock is enough to keep a vicar busy. Actually, I would prefer not to exploit my favored position in Society. I intend to find a small country vicarage on my own and work my way up on my own small merits."

"That's very—noble," she said.

Emma noticed that Nick was listening in on their conversation and directed a long, accusing look at him. She assumed Nick had coached his cousin to propriety, but he had done his work too well. James sounded like a stick-in-the-mud.

"I trust your clerical goals don't preclude dancing, Lord James?" she said, trying to lure him into more natural conversation. "Nick is having a rout party this evening in your honor."

"Oh, indeed, I have nothing against dancing. I'm not a Methodist. Every race indulges in the dance.

Anything so widespread must be natural to man. Though it is only our decadent society that has turned it into something lascivious. I am referring, of course, to the waltz."

Emma was rapidly losing interest in him. "Even the waltz can be done decorously," she said with a flouncing pout.

James's lips softened in a smile. When he replied, Emma sensed some ambiguity in his words. "Yes, it can, but why put temptation in man's way?"

His eyes were hot as they moved over the widow's stormy eyes and pouting lips. He noticed the fullness of her breasts and her dainty white hands. Self-restraint could only succeed so far. Human nature would out.

Nick sensed that the conversation was not going so well as he had hoped. He drew James into conversation with Hunter, and after he rose to fill his teacup, he sat beside Emma.

She gave him a long, questioning look. "Tell the truth, Nick. Did you put Lord James up to it?"

"Up to what?"

"To pretending he is some sort of saint or hermit?"

"Certainly not. What has he said?"

"You didn't mention that he intends to enter the church—and at the lowest level he can find."

"A few years ago he wanted to go and fight in the Peninsula. This year it's saving souls. James never does things by halves. He'd change his mind about the church, if a better offer came along."

"I don't plan to offer for him! I've learned my lesson."

"I should have said a better opportunity," Nick said, cursing his slip.

Emma gazed across the room at Lord James. She was intrigued by a gentleman who would want to don a shako and sword and kill men one year, and become a lowly vicar the next. A gentleman who condemned the waltz, yet who looked at a lady with fire glowing in his eyes. And who was young and handsome and nobly born besides.

"Well, what do you think of him?" Nick asked.

"He's fascinating," she said.

Nick looked at her uncertainly. "Are you practicing the art of dissimulation, or do you mean it?"

Her surprised look told him she was serious. "No, he really is fascinating. I look forward to knowing him better."

Nick's mind told him this was an excellent thing. It would be good for James, good for Emma, and good for himself to have a sensible neighbor. But the satisfaction and pleasure he expected wasn't there. In its place was a worm of discontent, as Emma gazed across at James with that faraway look in her eyes while he expounded some salutary tale on the evil of gambling to Mr. Hunter. That Mr. Hunter was listening to him with apparent interest was the greatest surprise of all.

"Of course, James is very young," Nick heard himself say. "Still wet behind the ears, really. His next notion may be to turn Whitehern into an orphanage or some such thing. One never knows what freakish start he'll come up with."

He expected a scold for having brought a gentleman of such unstable ways into her company, and after puffing him off as unexceptionable as well.

Emma smiled softly. "That's what is so fascinating about him. But don't worry that I would let him turn Whitehern into an orphanage. I have a little experience in handling gentlemen, you must know."

"I'm glad you like him," Nick said.

She tilted her head to one side and sat a moment,

thinking and darting glances at James, across the room. "I haven't said I liked him. I only said he's fascinating. Snakes are fascinating, too. It doesn't mean one approves, only that one is interested. He may prove too volatile for me to handle."

But the little smile at the corner of her lips told him she was looking forward to trying. Lord Hansard soon left, taking his cousin with him.

"We shall see you all this evening, then," he said, making his bows.

Lord James cast a long look at the widow and said in soft, caressing accents, "Perhaps I was a little hasty in condemning the waltz, Lady Capehart. As you said, it can be done decorously. Will you save me the waltzes?"

"I look forward to it, Lord James," she replied, and gave him her hand. He lifted it to his lips. Custom decreed that the hand should stop an inch below his lips. Emma thought perhaps it was James's gazing at her so intently that made him misjudge the distance, but his lips definitely grazed the back of her hand for a longish moment. When she felt a flicker of moisture on her flesh, she gave a start of alarm.

Hansard took James's elbow and said, "One would think you hadn't been fed!" and, in a thoroughly bad humor, led his cousin out the door. Nick was accustomed to having the waltzes with Emma. He had been looking forward to it.

As they drove home, Lord James chided gently, "You didn't warn me the widow is a beauty, Hansard. I was quite unprepared for it. I fear I may have misbehaved. It was kind of you to call my attention to my lapse, for I quite lost my head. It was her perfume, I think, that did it. That lovely scent of mimosa. A light-skirt I had under my protection last

65

year used that perfume. She was a hellion in bed. Mimosa acts like an aphrodisiac on my senses."

Nick gasped in astonishment. "A light-skirt? I heard nothing of this."

"Papa did an excellent job of hushing it up, as he always does."

"I'm packing you off home tomorrow, at dawn."

"Ah, Cousin, you wrong me. I am a changed man since my affair with Lily. I have learned the unwisdom of consorting with the muslin company. Only think, a child of mine being raised by a light-skirt."

"You got the woman enceinte?"

"So she would have me believe. At it turned out, she was three months pregnant when I first knew her—intimately. No, the child was not mine, but it might have been. It taught me a lesson. I have reformed. That is what decided me to enter the church and lead a life of sobriety, doing good to atone for the ills of my scarlet past."

As James was only twenty-two, Nick assumed he was not yet a hardened rake. He was young enough to change his ways. Marriage would be an excellent thing for him. "Whitehern is a very profitable estate," he said.

"Yes, and of more interest," James murmured, "did you notice that Lady Capehart's eyes, if I am not mistaken, had the leer of invitation?"

"Lady Capehart was not leering! She is a perfectly respectable widow, and I expect you to remember it."

"I shall certainly try, Hansard. I have a dreadful weakness for ladies, you know. I had hoped that daily doses of prayer might cure me, but prolonged abstinence is taking its toll. I am quite determined to behave myself, however. I shall go to my room when we return and read a few sermons by John Donne. Don't let me read his poems. They incite me to . . .

66

Ah, but you wouldn't understand. You are old and settled in your ways."

"I'm three and thirty. Not exactly Methuselah!"

"If you have lived so close to that enchantress all these years and not seduced her, you are invincible. How do you control your passions?"

"I bear in mind that I am a gentleman, and Lady Capehart is a lady."

"And a woman," James said softly. "I shall have her—in marriage, I mean. When confronted with two evils, I always choose the prettier."

"And the other evil?"

"Work, Cousin, in the field of the Lord, harvesting souls. I never really felt it was my calling. The jackets are so unbecoming, and all that fustian about truth and honesty. But with Lady Capehart by my side, I could be a saint in my own way."

Nick decided that he would give his young cousin a chance at reformation, but the lad would want watching. If he veered down the garden path, he would be dispatched home at once.

Nick spent a few moments in the stable speaking to his groom when they returned to Waterdown. Lord James said he would go to his room to read the sermons. When Nick went inside, he went to the library to hide the copy of John Donne's love poems. He couldn't find the book. He called his butler and asked about it.

"I believe you'll find Lord James has it, sir. He asked for it the moment he came in."

"Will you please tell him I need it, immediately."

Nick waited, pacing the length of the marble-floored hall while his butler went abovestairs. He told himself the churning in his stomach was due to the possibility of James offending Lady Capehart. It would be unconscionable if she were seduced by his cousin and houseguest. Really! Why hadn't Lady Revson warned him of this ungovernable streak in James?

The butler returned empty-handed. "It seems I was mistaken, your lordship. His lordship says it was John Donne's sermons that he borrowed from the library. Odd, as he borrowed them earlier and didn't return them," he added, with a raised eyebrow.

"Thank you, Simms," Nicholas said, and darted up to pound on James's door.

"Enter," Lord James called. "Ah, it is you, Nicholas, vigilant to prevent my falling into errant ways. What an excellent cousin you are."

He handed Nick the book of poems. "Unfortunately," Lord James said, "I have my favorite poems by heart. Perhaps if I apply myself diligently to the sermons, I shall overcome this weakness."

"You bloody well better!"

"I make you a solemn promise, Hansard, if I— forget myself with Lady Capehart, I shall do the right thing by her."

"Very kind of you!"

"Noblesse oblige," Lord James said, and smiling vaguely, he pulled the sermons out from under his pillow. "And now, if you would leave me, I shall apply myself to the sermons."

Chapter Nine

Emma didn't have time to get the green silk made up into a gown before the rout party. She had to wear one from before John's death. As he had liked her to cut a dash in Society, however, her greatest problem was deciding which of the many hanging in her closet to choose. After examining half a dozen possible choices, she chose a low-cut rose taffeta gown that was flattering to her raven hair and creamy skin. With it she wore the diamond necklace that had belonged to John's mama. It was not large, but the stones were particularly fine. They dazzled like concentrated rainbows around her creamy throat.

She felt a little pang of regret when her carriage wheeled up through the whispering oaks and elms of Hansard's park, with the hall rising in splendor against the purpling sky of twilight. It would have been fine to call Waterdown home, to stand in the entrance of the grandest home in the county by Lord Hansard's side, welcoming their guests.

His shocked "Marry *you*!" echoed in her ears. What had she been thinking of to offer for him?

As the party had been assembled on short notice, Lord Hansard was not having any guests to dinner before the rout. It occurred to him that he could ask Emma to be his hostess, but in a provincial society, that would lead to marital expectations. As the locals had two hosts that evening, they were well satisfied.

Hansard was almost sorry that Emma looked so ravishing when he greeted her. To see her back in colors after her long mourning carried him back to the first time he had met her, after her marriage to John. He had been astonished then that John had landed such an Incomparable and imagined future trouble for his aging neighbor with so extraordinarily beautiful a young wife. The trouble had never come during John's lifetime, but when he glanced at Lord James, he had a sinking sensation that it had arrived now. The loose-lipped smile on the young lord's face told clearly that he had forgotten all about the sermons of John Donne.

"You came!" James exclaimed in reverent accents, when Emma came forward to be welcomed.

Emma curtsied and said, "Good evening, Lord James." But she said it in a very satisfied way.

As the last guests straggled in, James said, "Let us begin the dancing with the waltzes, Cousin. It is not a formal ball, after all."

"No, let us not," Hansard replied through thin lips. "And I don't want you making a cake of yourself over Lady Capehart, James."

Nick was almost happy to note that Mr. Hunter had secured Emma for the first set. Any romantic menace he represented paled to insignificance beside the greater peril of the "fascinating" Lord James. Nick glanced around uneasily to see if James was misbehaving himself with any other lady, only to find him glued to the wall, watching Emma with a small, anticipatory smile on his handsome face, as patient as a cat lurking beneath a tree to catch a sparrow unaware. But as Nick glanced at Emma, he realized she was no sparrow. She was aware of

James's attention. Her coquettish glance flickered often in his direction.

William Bounty won Emma for the second set. When James made no move to stand up with any of the young girls who were ogling him, Nick took him by the elbow and led him away from the wall.

"This is a rout party, not a vigil," he said. "You will stand up with Miss Emery, and you will pretend to enjoy her company."

Lord James was stricken with remorse. "Was I being rude? Dreadfully sorry, Cousin, but how can a man be expected to do anything but stare when he is in the same room as *her*? I shall be vastly amusing to your Miss Emery to atone for my lapse. My, she's ugly, isn't she?"

James danced well and seemed to Nick to make a determined effort not to watch Emma—until the waltzes began. Then he was at her side so quickly one would think he had been shot from a pistol.

"At last!" he exclaimed, drawing her into his arms to whirl her about the floor like a caper merchant. He held her much too closely, he showered her with a hundred lavish compliments, and, as the music ended, he tucked her hand under his elbow and walked off to the refreshment parlor, where he had arranged with the butler to have a bottle of Nick's best champagne set aside for himself and Emma.

"Bring it to the library," he ordered, then led Emma down the marbled hall to this spacious chamber, with a servant following them with the wine.

One elderly couple sat by the grate. James settled Emma on a small sofa, well apart from them, snagged two glasses of champagne, and sat beside her.

"To us!" he toasted, adding very quickly and very

earnestly, "Do you believe in love at first sight, Lady Capehart?" he asked in his gentle voice.

"No. I believe in fascination at first sight."

"Surely that is redundant. Fascination is the casting of a spell at a glance—usually reserved for serpents, I believe. We have fascinated each other, *ça va sans dire*. What we must discover is whether it is love."

She disliked that charge of mutual fascination, but decided not to challenge it. "We shan't discover that in one evening, Lord James," she said instead.

"Lord me no lords, and I shall lady you no ladies. Jamie and Emma. It is much too soon for it, but I feel I have known you forever . . . in my dreams." He touched his glass to hers and drank. "The names have a certain *je ne sais quoi*. Euphonious, if not mellifluous."

"Let us not rush rashly into things, Lord James."

"Ah, I see Cupid's arrow has not cut so deeply into your heart as into mine. But it has nicked you, Emma. Say it has. You feel something for me."

"We shall see about that," she said, but an encouraging smile peeped out to belie her show of reluctance.

He smiled, satisfied. "I daresay a lady likes to put up a token show of resistance. It is odd that my own back is not arched, for usually when I am dispatched about the country to seek a bride, I dig in my heels and dislike everything about the lady concerned. I came prepared to find you provincial and ugly, and instead I found—perfection." He drew his fingers to his lips and kissed them.

"And were you dispatched to Waterdown for the express purpose of courting me?" she asked in a calm voice that concealed her curiosity.

"It was rather a case of being summoned on this

occasion. The summons came from Hansard. 'A wealthy, impatient widow in need of a husband,' he said. What he did not say was that you are an Aphrodite."

"I see," she said, and took a sip of her wine while she digested this. "Impatient widow!" He made her sound desperate for a man. She couldn't decide whether to be angry with Nick or amused at his simple plan,

Nick had seen Jámes lead Emma toward the refreshment parlor. He felt they would be safe there for a few minutes, but uncertainty soon sent him pelting off after them. When he saw they weren't there, he flew into alarm.

"Have you seen Lord James?" he asked the servant behind the table.

"His lordship had a bottle of champagne taken to the library, milord."

"Did he indeed!" His best champagne no doubt, the scoundrel! He darted off to the library, hardly knowing what he might find, only to see Emma and James sitting quietly at the side of the room, with an elderly couple seated by the grate to play propriety. He slowed his pace as he walked toward the sofa.

"Well, and what are you up to?" he asked.

"We were just discussing love," James replied.

"At first sight," Emma added with a glinting smile. "Or should I say at first reading?" Nick realized James had revealed the letter dispatched to Lady Revson.

"Emma doesn't believe in it," James said. "She says it is only fascination. It would be interesting to hear an older gentleman's opinion on the matter. What do you think, Cousin? Draw up a chair and give us the benefit of your decades of experience among the petticoats."

Nick's jaw tightened. "Decades of experience" indeed! He made him sound like an old lecher.

"I think such deep, philosophical discussions shouldn't be held at a rout party. I threw this do to introduce you to the local Society, James. You aren't meeting anyone in here."

"I am meeting with everyone who matters to me—Emma," James replied, with a languishing look at her.

"Hansard is right," Emma said. "We shall continue this fascin—this discussion—another time."

Lord James laughed softly. "The heart is quicker than the tongue. I, too, found it fascinating, Emma. À demain." He rose, touched her fingers once more, and bowed.

Nick assisted Emma from the sofa, took a firm grip on her elbow, and ushered her out of the room. "I wouldn't encourage him," he said, rather grimly.

"Strange, I thought that was exactly what you hoped for, since you summoned him here to court me."

"Is that what he said?"

"Do you deny it?"

"If I had realized he was such a loose screw I never would have invited him."

"The man is a menace. He could talk a cow out of her calf."

"I hope he hasn't been—annoying you?"

"Oh no! I am seldom annoyed when a gentleman finds me irresistible. It is quite a novelty for me. And I had to overcome a severe handicap as well. Jamie usually digs in his heels and bucks when he is sent off to court a lady."

"Jackass!"

"You are too hard on yourself, Nick."

"I didn't mean me!"

"Oh, sorry."

74

He glared. "He mentioned seeing you tomorrow. It would be unwise to go off alone with him. He's been reading John Donne." Emma frowned. "Don't ask," he said wearily.

At the door of the ballroom, Emma stopped. "You brought him here in the hope of making a match between us, Nick. Now that your plan shows some sign of success, you seem unhappy with the notion."

"The boy's an idiot!"

"There is that, but he's rather a sweet idiot," she said with a forgiving smile. "I think I can lead him. He seems biddable. And as you said yourself, his papa is an earl; Lord James has expectations, and there is the family mansion in London. . . ."

Nick hardly knew what to say. It was all true. James had expressed an interest in marriage, not an affair. Surely an excess of passion for one's intended bride should be no deterrent to a happy marriage. Yet he was deeply dissatisfied with the notion of James marrying Emma. The boy was unstable, he told himself. He'd soon tire of his bride and be haring off after other girls.

"I thought you were in no hurry to marry," he said.

"Oh, I am not in a hurry—unless I hear Aunt Hildegarde is on her way, despite the leaking roof," she added, for she was enjoying Nick's discomfort.

Nick had the cotillion with Emma, but it was James who escorted her to dinner. He also secured her company for the country dances that came later. That rowdy affair gave little opportunity for dalliance, however, and he behaved himself moderately well.

Nick and James went to the door to say good night to the parting guests.

"Will seven tomorrow be too early for me to call?" James asked, clutching Emma's hand.

"Seven?" Emma exclaimed. "Why—it is almost too late, if you wish to ride or drive."

"Ah, you misunderstand me, Emma. I meant seven in the morning."

Her lips quirked in a smile. "That is a little early for me. Shall we say, ten?"

"But that is eight hours away!"

"Well, we have to sleep," she pointed out.

"True, but not together."

"James!" Nick cried.

"Sorry, Cuz," he said perfunctorily, then he returned his besotted gaze to Emma. "To sleep, perchance to dream . . ."

"Say good night, James," Nick said through clenched lips.

"Parting is such sweet sorrow," Emma said, and blew them both a kiss. The silver tinkle of her laughter wafted on the air behind her.

"She really is something special." James sighed. "My inclination, if not my judgment, nudges me toward the altar."

"Then your judgment is at fault. She is worlds too good for you."

"True. I shall put my faith in my inclination in this case. How shall I ever thank you for calling her to my attention, Cuz?"

"You might begin by not acting like a demmed fool."

"Oh, but the ladies like that, you know. Better than scowling at 'em as I notice you do. No need to act so barbarous and surly. Remember Seneca's question, Hansard. 'When shall we live, if not now?' All your scowls haven't gotten you a wife, and you're middle-aged. But you're not too old a dog to learn a new trick."

"When I want a wife, I won't have to resort to

trickery to win her," Nick said, and strode off angrily to his study to solemnly ponder James's puerilities. Barbarous? Surly? Middle-aged? Bah! What did that unlicked cub know about love? He only wanted to bed Emma. This hardly improved his mood or lessened the need for vigilance.

Chapter Ten

James was an eager suitor, but he was not a cagey one. He made the error of asking Nick, the next morning, where the most romantic ride on his estate was to be found.

"Emma mentioned riding or driving," he said. "Riding lends itself better to forwarding our friendship than driving. The ladies always want to go to a village and poke about the shops."

"Emma likes riding," Nick replied, thinking this a relatively harmless pastime. "Try the west meadow. You'll find fences and ditches there."

"That sounds excellent for riding. You and I must go there one day, but for dalliance, I envision a babbling brook, surrounded by trees, with a small area of soft grass, away from view of any chance passerby. Flowers would be nice, wildflowers for choice, to perfume the air."

Nick bit back his anger and said curtly, "Emma likes to ride in her own spinney and meadows. My brook hasn't been landscaped for seduction."

"You really ought to do something about that, Cousin. It wouldn't be much trouble. I daresay there are willows growing there. One seldom sees a brook without willows nearby. You could lop down a couple of them and plant grass. Or better, sweet clover, starred with wildflowers."

"Why not a bed?" Nick asked sarcastically.

James considered it a moment. "Too obvious. A grassy bank makes a pliant mattress."

When the troublesome guest took to the roof after breakfast with a telescope, Nick had a fair notion he was scouting out a spot to romance Emma. He had a fair notion which spot James would choose, too. There was a clearing by the brook, such as he had mentioned, on Emma's property. Nick gave them twenty minutes' lead, at which time he headed for the brook. He found them right where he expected, but there was nothing amiss with their behavior.

They sat side by side, laughing and talking. James was making a daisy chain for Emma. She already wore a flower diadem on her head. She had removed her bonnet, and James his curled beaver. A daisy was stuck in the rim of the latter. Neither of them seemed surprised or dismayed to see him.

"Nick," Emma said, glancing up. She looked lovely, with a soft light glowing in her eyes and a gentle smile on her lips. If she wasn't in love, she wasn't far from it.

"I found the ideal spot!" James said. "When I told Emma what I had in mind—don't stare like that! I promised her I would behave. Anyhow, she knew the very place. It even has flowers. Emma has never made a daisy chain. Imagine!"

Nick dismounted and joined them. "Odd you didn't know of this spot, Cousin," James said mischievously.

"I'm not so familiar with Lady Capehart's property as I am with my own."

"It's perfectly idyllic," James said, looking all around at the flower-spangled grass and the babbling brook. "One would hardly be surprised to see Echo and Narcissus loitering here amidst the woodland nymphs."

Nick said, "If you're through with that daisy chain, I thought I might give you a tour of the estate, James."

"Emma's or your own?" James inquired.

"Waterdown," Nick said.

"Ah, I thought perhaps as Whitehern had been held out as a lure—Don't blush, Hansard, Emma is familiar with your scheme. I believe in honesty in my dealings."

Nick was aware of Emma's laughing face without looking at her. She was enjoying his embarrassment! "Honesty is one word for it," he said dampingly.

"And indiscretion is another," James added, nodding. "Perhaps you're right. I do tend to indiscretion. Very well, Hansard. I shall join you, after we accompany Emma home. We can't very well leave her here alone. I am always interested to tour estates. One never knows, I might have one myself one day. You, for instance, are still single and have no son to leave Waterdown to."

"I haven't given up hope," Nick said.

They accompanied Emma, still wearing her daisy chain and carrying her flower wreath, to her home.

"Until this evening, Emma," James said, when they reached the stable. He lifted her down from her mount with style and agility, whirling her in the air to reveal her lace-edged petticoat and her dainty ankles.

When Emma's feet were back on the ground, she glanced at Nick. "I hope you will join us for dinner as well, Nick," she said.

"I tentatively accepted on both our behalfs," James told his host.

"Then it seems the matter has been settled without consulting me," Nick said, rather brusquely.

He was aware that he was being surly, but some

demon drove him to it. It was seeing James and Emma together, on such close terms after only twenty-four hours. At this rate she'd be shackled to the wretched boy before they had come to know each other—and it was all his fault.

Nick determined that he'd be more civil at dinner that evening. But when he saw the corsage James had fashioned to take to Emma, he felt such a surge of vexation that he could hardly control it.

"I arranged these rosebuds and forget-me-nots and fern fronds into a corsage for her," James said, smiling at the pretty thing.

"Weren't a head wreath and a daisy chain enough?" Nick asked.

"Can there ever be enough of beauty, Cousin?" James asked, in a chiding spirit.

The romance continued apace over dinner. The lovers exchanged soft glances over the turbot and smiles over the saddle of mutton. It was while the gentlemen were taking their port after dinner that Nick began to wonder just how serious James's talk of reformation was.

"I shall be taking a spin into the village after port, if you're interested, Lord James," Derek said. "There's a card game at the local inn."

"Women?" James asked with a certain eagerness.

Derek Hunter looked askance at Hansard. "I daresay something might be arranged if you're interested."

"I'm interested," James said, then turned to Nick. "I mustn't let myself get too worked up, you know, Nick, or I might misbehave with Emma. It is only out of consideration for her that I inquired for a light-skirt. After we marry I shall be as faithful as Darby with his Joan. Will you come along with us?"

"I think not."

James nodded. "Mrs. Pettigrew. Mama mentioned she had settled nearby. I wondered what you did for a woman. She's very handsome."

Nick poured himself another glass of port and said nothing. Not only did he want to spare Mrs. Pettigrew James's attentions, but he didn't want to have two ladies to guard against this fascinating young lecher.

After taking their port, the gentlemen joined the ladies in the saloon for three-quarters of an hour, at which time James and Hunter took their leave.

"Mr. Hunter has invited me to a game of cards in the village," James explained.

"You are perfectly welcome to play here," Emma offered.

James smiled fondly. "How could I concentrate on cards, when you are near?"

Rather than risk further rebuff in front of Nick, she allowed him to get away with this sophistry.

After they left Miss Foxworth opened her novel, and Emma turned a wary eye on Nick.

"I hope Derek isn't leading Lord James into mischief," she said. "Heaven knows what he gets up to at the Rose and Thistle."

"They're young," Nick said forgivingly. "Young men need their diversions."

"The stakes are deep there, you know," she said, frowning. "If James is a gambler, I shan't have him."

"I shouldn't rush into anything, if I were you. You spoke of going to London. Why don't you go?"

Her lips drew into that pout that Nick found so enticing. She spoke in a low voice to avoid Miss Foxworth's attention. "Derek hasn't mentioned it since I refused his offer."

"You don't have to go with Hunter. Indeed, he is the last person you should go with."

"I can't very well go alone. With only Miss Foxworth, I mean. We are both green as grass. I've only stayed at a hotel three times in my whole life. Twice with John and once with Papa."

Nick knew Emma wasn't a sophisticated woman, but this speech made him realize what a protected life she had led. She had gone from her father's provincial home to an even more secluded life at Whitehern. No wonder she had fallen for James. He really should introduce her to some decent *partis*. These, alas, were only to be met in London. She would indeed be easily taken advantage of in London without someone to guide her. He owed it to John, he told himself.

"It happens I'll be going myself the day after tomorrow," he said, inventing the trip on the spot.

She looked definitely interested. "As Lord James has come especially to become acquainted with me, it seems wrongheaded for me to leave at this time."

Nick said the only thing he could say. "I'm sure James would be happy to come with us." Hopefully he would find other Incomparables to entertain him once they were there.

A smile of pure enchantment beamed. "That would be lovely, Nick! You must tell me what hotel is respectable—but not too dear."

It wasn't an undue concern for thrift that caused the speech. Emma was wealthy, but she didn't really have any notion of the value of money. John used to use the excuse of London being expensive to keep her at Whitehern.

"As Miss Foxworth will be with you, there's no reason you shouldn't stay with me on Berkeley Square," he said. "Actually it happens my aunt Gertrude is there at the moment, doing some shopping,

83

I'm told. We'll be doubly chaperoned. That is—you and James will be well chaperoned."

"I hardly think we require two female chaperons when you keep such a sharp eye on us," she said, and gave him a questioning look. "It wasn't by chance that you joined us this morning, I think?"

He gave a rueful smile. "I was a little concerned, when he inquired for a spot hidden from any stray passerby. I feel responsible, as I'm the one who brought him here."

"That's very thoughtful of you, Nick. John used to watch out for me like that. But you needn't worry about James. I can keep him in line. Do you think he means half the pretty things he says?"

"Yes, half of them."

She drew a deep sigh. "It's very difficult finding a good husband. I'm glad I have you to help me."

"I'm glad I could be of assistance. The Season is over, but there will still be plenty of company in town. I'm sure we'll find a few routs and parties where I can introduce you to some eligible gentlemen. You haven't met anyone like James before. I think you're merely bowled over by his—charm," he said, hesitating over the word.

"Yes, he is charming, but I'm not sure he would wear well. How would he stand up during any difficulty? I remember how you and John took control so quickly when that horrid hoof-and-mouth disease struck the herd. I cannot see James being so capable. One must think of the bad times as well as the good. For better or for worse, as the marriage ceremony says. John was wonderful during the worse times, but he didn't really know how to enjoy the better."

As she had already linked John's name with his own, Nick felt this speech, both the good and the bad, applied to him as well.

"Not that I mean to disparage John!" she added quickly. "I think it was probably his age, so much older than myself, that caused it. I expect that is half the attraction James has for me. He's young. He doesn't think of anything bad ever happening, probably because nothing bad ever has happened to him. He thinks of life as one long, sunny summer afternoon."

Nick listened and noted that, though Emma was young and unworldly, she wasn't foolish. Someone, probably that Aunt Hildegarde and the papa she denigrated, had pounded some wisdom into her.

He heard himself mouthing the boring cliché, "Into every life some rain must fall."

She shook her head and said, "Goodness, how did we manage to tumble into such a serious conversation when we started out talking about London? Now, tell me what delights await us when the Season is not in progress."

The remainder of the visit passed more pleasantly. Emma listened entranced as he spoke of the plays and parties and shops awaiting them. Even Miss Foxworth joined in the conversation.

"Derek will like that," she said.

Nick and Emma exchanged a startled glance. They had forgotten about Derek Hunter. Nick saw the visit turning into a mass invasion of his London home. He had wanted to get Emma away from her unsuitable suitors, but it seemed they would accompany her to London.

Emma's smile faded, her lips drooped, and she said, "Perhaps we should make it some other time, Nick."

"Nonsense," Nick said. "We'll all go. You can't abandon your houseguest."

As he drove home he was hard put to account for having involved himself in this scheme. It could not possibly be anything but a prolonged headache. He had pitched himself—and Emma—from the frying pan into the fire. London offered a good many more chances for James to misbehave than Whitehern did.

Emma was also surprised at his generosity. In the end she decided that Nick must be doing it to foster the new romance. Having brought James and herself together, he wanted to show her a true, balanced picture of her suitor. He drew her attention to James's little faults, as he had mentioned the advantages to the match earlier. Nick was the sort of gentleman who would do that. Just so would John have behaved, had he been here. She decided she had underestimated Nick. He did care for her. Not as a lover, but as a friend. It was nice to have a good friend, especially at this critical time in her life.

Chapter Eleven

"Very kind of Hansard," Derek said, when Emma told him of the invitation to London. He had never before been invited to visit such a tonish establishment as Hansard House. He was thoroughly aware of the honor and strongly inclined to accept, but common sense told him a gentleman would be seen as cadging if he stayed in another man's house when he had a place of his own in the same city. Then too, the visit was only for a short while. Emma might expect him to remain in London when it was over, whereas he planned to make an extended stay at Whitehern. By September, he felt, he would have exhausted the town's resources and be ready to move on. All things considered, he was very well situated at Whitehern for the nonce, even without his hostess.

"I've been thinking, Emma," he continued. "Why don't I stay here and keep an eye on things while you're away? Someone of the family, you see, to keep the servants and that bailiff of yours on their toes."

"That's not necessary. My bailiff has been with us for years, but if you would like to remain here, then by all means, do so." She gave him a wary look, fearful of offending him, yet determined to protect her home. "But no wild parties, mind. No women and no gambling for heavy stakes."

"I promise," he said, perfectly unoffended. "This is dashed good of you, Emma." Then he remembered he had put the notion forward as a favor to her and added, "I shall keep a sharp eye on everything for you. About a carriage . . ."

"As I shall be going in Hansard's carriage, I would be grateful if you would exercise my team from time to time."

"That will be no trouble at all," he said, grinning from ear to ear.

Lord James also had a few reservations about the visit. "You're doing it on purpose, Cousin. You think I'm not good enough for Emma and are planning to throw other *partis* in her path," he charged.

"Would I invite you to join us if that were the case?"

"You could hardly do anything else. You are a gentleman, after all, and I am an invited guest at your home. But you shan't keep us apart. I can hold my own against all comers where my Emma is concerned."

"Then you'll be joining us?"

"Certainly I shall, but I must have a word with a certain Fifi at the Rose and Thistle before we leave. I have an arrangement with her for the evenings. A charming chit, by the by. When you're ready for a change from Mrs. Pettigrew, I highly recommend Fifi."

"Yes, I can tell by the name she's a charmer," Nick said with a look of loathing.

The travel arrangements were made; Lord Hansard notified his London household of his plans, and two mornings later his traveling carriage left for London, carrying Emma, Mrs. Foxworth, Lord James, and himself. Derek Hunter waved them off with a slight pang. It would have been something, staying at Hansard House. Then he borrowed Sir John's gun and mount and rode out to enjoy a spot of hunting.

The trip to London, in a well-sprung carriage drawn by a team of deep-chested matched bays, was enjoyable on a spring day. By leaving in the morning, they arrived late in the afternoon. As they drew into the city, Emma lodged her nose against the carriage window and goggled like the veriest Johnnie Raw.

"So many people!" she exclaimed, staring at drovers and pedestrians and ramshackle commercial establishments, eking out a living for their proprietors on the fringes of the city. "It's not very elegant, is it? I expected it to be grander."

"This is only the outskirts," Lord James informed her.

When the carriage entered the purlieus of the West End, the grandness Emma anticipated was there in full measure. Stately homes sat behind iron fences, looking out on the broad cobbled streets. Windows sparkled, brass door knockers positively gleamed. Elegant carriages of all sorts went to and fro. Landaus, barouches, chaises, curricles, and high-perch phaetons, some of them driven by ladies, wheeled past, lending a lively touch to the scene. Footmen in assorted shades of livery darted about, looking more haughty than the lords and ladies they served.

"It is just as I imagined." Emma sighed. "Which house is yours, Nick?"

"The next block."

The carriage soon pulled up in front of one of the stately brick houses. The house was not so large or so grand as Waterdown, but it was in the very heart of polite London. The butler admitted them to a carved hall, with doorways like triumphal arches leading to

89

grand chambers beyond. Overhead was a massive girandole hung with cut-glass lusters, beneath their feet a glistening floor of scagliola.

Emma entered with her heart pounding to be welcomed by Lady Gertrude Philmore, a more noble version of Miss Foxworth. It was difficult to assimilate at first that this hawk-nosed dame in the elegant mauve gown with a huge amethyst at her throat was another romantic, but so it was.

She called for tea to refresh the travelers, showed them into Lord Hansard's elegant saloon, and demanded roguishly, "And which of you is the gentleman who is in love with Lady Capehart, eh?"

James smiled softly. "It is I, Auntie. Have I not chosen well?"

"I knew it! So romantic. But it cannot be a runaway match, or Nick would not be here."

"Oh, we might manage to escape him," James said mischievously.

"Don't put ideas in his head!" Nick exclaimed. He glanced at Emma to see the laughter glinting in her eyes.

The travelers were tired from the trip, so it was decided the ladies would rest until dinnertime, and the party would attend Drury Lane that evening. Lady Gertrude, who had already seen the performance twice, declined. Nick had a box for the Season, but with the Season just over, he had to send out for tickets. As the box held six, he wrote to invite his eligible bachelor friend, Lord Sanichton, to join them and bring his sister along.

In her room Emma found it impossible to rest. She examined the fine furnishings of her bedchamber—the bed hangings of rich blue and gold brocade, the Persian carpet, the carved mahogany dresser—and was glad she wasn't staying at some impersonal and vastly expensive hotel. She went to the window and sighed in pleasure at the busy street below. This was the life! And this evening she would be attending the fabled Drury Lane Theater to see a production of *Romeo and Juliet*.

Mr. Milmont had never allowed his family to attend the theater, which he called Satan's parlor. Thus Emma had never seen *Romeo and Juliet*. She read a good deal, but found Shakespeare's archaic language too daunting to tackle alone. Even without reading it, however, she knew the play to be the quintessential romance and looked forward to seeing it with the keenest pleasure.

She had brought with her her most fashionable gowns. For the theater she selected an Empire style gown of sea green. Its silken underskirt was covered with a fuller skirt of gauze, edged in Belgian lace that billowed about her green kid slippers like foam. At her creamy throat, a diamond and emerald necklace sparkled. She piled her silken curls on top of her head, fastening them with jeweled combs. She felt like a princess when she went belowstairs for dinner.

"Venus, rising from the waves!" Lord James exclaimed, when he greeted her at the bottom of the stairs, where he was lurking in anticipation of her descent. "I feared you would not have any gowns stylish enough for London, but I might have known!"

Emma accepted this ambiguous compliment with good grace. Nick, chewing back a smile, said, "I, on the other hand, had no doubt about the gown. Emma is famous for her fashions, James."

James laughed. "Can one find fame among the barns and ricks of Sussex? She was ogled by the provincials, you mean. *Now* she will be famous. I shall be proud to be seen in public with you, Emma," he said, taking her fingers and squeezing them. "In fact, I feel I ought to propose to you this instant, before some more worthy suitor steals you away from me."

"You look very nice, too, Lord James," she said. She noticed that James's coiffure had been rearranged à la Titus, and his modest cravat was worn in a more complicated style. His plain dark jacket had given way to a bottle green one that lent him a touch of sophistication.

"You noticed," he said, placing a kiss on her palm. "If I am not to be a clergyman, there is no need to dress the part. I am so glad. I feel those dreary duds did me less than justice, so I sent to Papa's house for a few things. Come, let us dine."

They dined *en famille*, a pleasant but not ostentatious meal. The silver and china, the food and wine were all of the best, without soaring to Olympian heights of refinement.

Soon after dinner Lord Sanichton and Lady Margaret came to accompany them to the theater. Emma noticed that Lord Sanichton was cut from the same mold as Nick. He was older than James, and more sensible. She thought him quite good looking, though perhaps not quite what she would call handsome. He was a few inches short of six feet. His shoulders were broad, his hair was chestnut, and his features were well arranged.

His sister, while younger, was a little old to still be on the shelf. Emma thought it was her somewhat gaunt figure that accounted for it. At five and twenty she was very much a lady of the town. Her gown, her coiffure, her easy manners—everything about her spoke of the ton.

They had a glass of wine, then left for the theater. Nick led Miss Foxworth to his carriage and suggested that Emma accompany Sanichton and Lady

Margaret in their rig. James took it for granted that he would accompany Emma and tagged along with her. The ladies sat together on one banquette and ignored the gentlemen.

"Nick tells me this is your first trip to London," Lady Margaret said. "You must let me show you about."

"*I* am to be Lady Capehart's escort," Lord James informed her.

"Of course you are, James, but I am referring to modistes and milliners and coiffeurs and such things that would bore a gentleman."

"I have never found them boring. Quite the contrary, but as I still owe several of them money for past favors, we accept your offer."

Lady Margaret lifted an eyebrow at Emma, as if to say, "Is this outrageous sprig your fiancé?" Emma smiled and shook her head. For the remainder of the trip, Lady Margaret outlined the shops that must be visited. Sanichton was impressed with Lady Capehart's ready smile. Nor was he put off by her frequent interruptions.

"Did you see that!" she exclaimed, when a gentleman driving three horses tandem shot past.

"That must be the Prince Regent at least!" she cried, when a particularly fine blue carriage drawn by a snow white team pulled past.

"Actually, I believe that's Miss Drew," Margaret said, smiling at her brother. They both recognized the famous courtesan.

When, at last, they reached Drury Lane Theater, Emma gasped in delight. Torches illuminated the marble and porphyry exterior, lending it the air of a fairy castle.

"It's like a temple! I have never seen anything so grand!" she exclaimed, when she was led into the lobby. Along its sixty-foot length of faux porphyry, plaster statues in imitation of marble originals rose in stately splendor above the plush sofas. Uniformed page boys darted to and fro among the early arrivals, outfitted in finery to challenge their surroundings.

"A theater has much in common with a church, or temple," James said, gazing about with a cynical eye. "Both give performances to entertain the jaded masses."

Emma didn't hear him. She was frowning at a set of water pipes and great brass water cocks that seemed incongruous in this setting.

"Those are to insure that the theater doesn't burn down again," James told her. "Actually, they are the only authentic things in the lobby. The rest of it is sham finery in the worst of bad taste. But I am glad it pleases you, Emma," he added, with no notion of casting aspersions on her taste.

He led her to their box, seated Emma in the front row, and sat beside her. Nick nudged Sanichton into the seat on Emma's other side. He need not have worried that Emma would fall into a flirtation with James. She was so entranced by the play that she didn't shift her gaze from the stage until the first intermission, and then it was only to praise the performance and gawk about at the audience.

"I hadn't realized there were so many rich people in the whole kingdom," she said, marveling at the sparkle of jewels and the sheen of silks and satins. "There must be thousands of people here."

"The theater holds twenty-eight hundred. Perhaps twenty-eight of them are actually wealthy," James informed her. "The rest of us are here to provide an audience for the twenty-eight."

"It is almost as good as the play onstage," Emma

said. It was the way she had dreamed London would be, all those years at home, pining for it.

At the second intermission, Lady Margaret drew her out into the corridor to ogle those who were having wine and walking about to stretch their legs. Lord James made a quick dart to the greenroom to try his hand at meeting the actress who was playing Lady Capulet. She was half again as old as himself, but not too old to be of amorous interest. She had a well-preserved figure.

Nick was not tardy in pushing Sanichton forward as his friend had expressed a warm interest in the young widow.

"I don't want to interfere if she and James—"

"That is exactly why we are here, to introduce Lady Capehart to some eligible *partis*. James has her in his eye."

"He would, of course. Pity he dropped in on you and discovered her. He is exactly the sort of here-and-therein you would not want her to meet, if you feel some responsibility for Lady Capehart. You heard about his fracas with the actress?"

Nick felt doubly guilty for having encouraged Lord James. "I heard nothing of it until James told me himself, after I had invited him to Waterdown."

"It occurred in early April, before the Season opened. His papa had to come down heavy to rescue him, I believe, but it seemed for a while that it did the lad some good. I heard he had reformed his ways. It don't look like it now, however. He darted back to the greenroom between acts. What are Lady Capehart's feelings for him?"

"She's interested, but by no means has decided to have him. She's not a fool after all. I hope to introduce her to some more plausible gents."

"In that case, put me at the top of your list!"

"You're already there, Sanichton," Nick said.

Sanichton smiled. "I'm off then. You amuse Maggie, will you?"

Nick dutifully joined Lady Margaret, but when he saw Sanichton tuck Emma's hand under his elbow, he felt again that worm of discontent. A little gnawing, nagging worry that something was not quite as it should be. What could it be? There was nothing amiss with Sanichton. He was an excellent fellow and would make a fine landlord for Whitehern. Of course, he would not live there himself. He had his own larger estate in Devonshire, but he would keep an eye on it, see it was well run.

Nick shook away the wisp of worry and applied himself to the task of entertaining Lady Margaret. When they returned to their box, Emma said quietly in Nick's ear, "I like your Lord Sanichton. I am to drive out with him tomorrow afternoon. Does that please you?"

"Very much," Nick said, but he had to force a smile.

Lord James returned late to the box, wearing a suspiciously smug expression, and disappeared entirely after the performance. James always could be counted on to bite the hand that fed him. He had arranged to meet Lady Capulet and join a little party that was going out to eat and drink.

"You will see that Emma gets home safely, Nick," he said. "She looks so ravishing this evening that I cannot trust myself with her."

"Don't fall into a scrape with your new actress friend," Nick cautioned. "Your papa won't pull you out a second time."

James took offense at this little lecture. "I've learned my lesson," he said. "It is perfectly safe. She's married."

That being the case, Nick offered no further instructions. When he went to offer Emma his arm, he found her hiding in a dark corner, with tears flowing freely down her cheeks. The only thing he could think of was that she and James had had a tiff. He sat beside her, to conceal her grief from Sanichton.

"Emma," he said, putting his arm around her shoulders. "He's not worth it, my dear. Come, the rest of us will go out for supper."

She sniffled and accepted the handkerchief he pushed into her fingers. "Oh, it was awful, Nick. I had no idea."

"What the devil did he say to you?"

"To me? Nothing. How should he speak to me?"

"Then what—"

"It's them," she said, nodding toward the stage, where the curtain had already closed for the last time. "I didn't know they *died*! What a wretched takein. I thought *Romeo and Juliet* was supposed to be a romance. It's a horrid tragedy."

Nick bit back a wry smile and blotted away her tears. It struck him that Emma was as innocent and foolish as Juliet. He felt an urge to take her in his arms and tell her it was going to be all right.

"It's only a play, Emma," he said gently. "Romeo and Juliet will be back on the boards tomorrow night, to die again and rise like a pair of phoenixes."

Her lips trembled open in a watery smile. "You're right, of course. You must think me a goose." She peered at him uncertainly. "Could we come back and see it again before we leave?"

"If you like."

A radiance of pure joy shone on her upturned face. "Oh, I would love it of all things! I have never seen anything like it. And now let us go for that dinner. Crying always makes me hungry. I'm ravenous."

"A lady is never ravenous," he told her. "Peckish is the greatest hunger permitted to her."

"Oh dear. I fear I'm giving Lord Sanichton a very poor opinion of me. I noticed he and his sister exchanging smiles when I mistook Miss Drew's carriage for the Prince Regent's."

"Sanichton has nothing against innocence. Nor have I," he added, and led her out to the waiting carriage.

Chapter Twelve

It was arranged that Lord Sanichton would take Lady Capehart for a visitor's tour of London the next afternoon. Hansard would accompany them, along with Lady Margaret. Emma chose her most stylish day gown of jonquil jaconet with a pointed lace collar. She tilted her yellow chipped-straw hat over her eye and carried a silk umbrella against the sun, which might possibly show its shy face before they returned.

As Lord James had not returned home the preceding evening, it was unknown what plans he might be hatching. When he showed up for luncheon that day, tired and drawn from his amorous exertions, he was in the boughs to learn of what he called Hansard's "betrayal."

"After summoning me to Waterdown to nab Emma, you pull this stunt on me, dropping Sanichton in over my head the moment my back is turned. That sheep in sheep's clothing! As if Emma would care for him. It is infamous, Cousin! You shan't get away with it. I shall join you in the outing. And by the by, it is a perfectly wretched afternoon you have planned. Just what one would expect of you and Sanichton. No one but gluttons for punishment would want to see the Tower of London and the Exeter Exchange and St. Paul's *again*."

"Emma has never seen them," Hansard pointed out.

"I look forward to it with pleasure," Emma said.

James looked at her askance. "A dead bore, I promise you. A dose of laudanum is nothing to them. Ah well, I daresay it is one's duty to see dull monuments once, but I doubt they warrant a special visit. Tomorrow I shall show you *my* London." Hansard trembled to think what this young rake's London might consist of, but James spoke on to reassure him. "Emma and I prefer nature, you must know. Gardens, parks, perhaps a ride in Rotten Row."

"That sounds delightful," Emma said. Hansard could not in good conscience object, and peace was restored.

Rather than break up the party, it was decided to crowd five into Lord Sanichton's carriage for the tour. James, being the slightest man, sat between the ladies and tried in vain to seize Emma's fingers. When this failed he tried for Lady Margaret's and was again thwarted, though the dame was delighted with his efforts, especially when Hansard smiled conspiratorially at her predicament.

After they alighted at the Exeter Exchange, James took Emma's left elbow, Sanichton her right, and they set off, with Lady Margaret and Hansard following behind.

"There is nothing worth seeing here but the wild animals," James said, and insisted on curtailing the visit to this trivial show. "It is the fashion to say the hippopotamus resembles Lord Liverpool," he said derisively. "Anyone with an eye in his head can see the hippo is first cousin to Prinney. From the rear, I mean. The creature's face is not quite so grotesque as our Prince Regent's. More like Princess Mary's."

The hippo obligingly turned and trotted off, its fat rump waddling. "There! Put a pair of inexpressibles on it and you have Prince George!" James announced, in a carrying voice that won him a few cold stares. "Well, we have done Exeter Exchange. St. Paul's cathedral is next. You will find Wren's boring domes scattered all over London. When you have seen St. Paul's, you have seen them all."

At St. Paul's Lord Sanichton refused to be bulloxed into viewing only the exterior. He escorted Emma inside and spoke at length about the cathedral's marvels, not just mentioning its dome and pillars and windows, but expatiating fully on the price of its construction.

"Seven hundred and fifty thousand pounds, and that was in the seventeenth century, mind. It was paid for by a tax on sea-borne coal."

James yawned ostentatiously into his fist. Emma listened with half an ear, the rest of her attention on the magnificent architecture. She noticed that Hansard had led Lady Margaret on ahead to view the altar. He was pointing out features of interest to her as they went up the aisle. Emma also noticed that Lady Margaret's face was quite radiant with pleasure at Hansard's attentions. Was there something between them?

Westminster Abbey was also on their list, and again Sanichton seemed to find interest in the less magnificent aspects of the place. He lingered at the coronation chair, which struck Emma as a very insignificant piece of furniture for such a glorious occasion. There was no gilt, no upholstery, and the carving was crude. She had finer chairs herself at Whitehern.

James was awaiting them when they went outside. The clergyman manqué had had enough of ecclesiastical architecture for one day.

"Now may we go and visit a garden?" he asked.

"God is not to be found inside on such a day as this. He is out enjoying the sun and flowers and pretty ladies."

"We shall look at the Houses of Parliament while we are nearby," Sanichton decreed. "Lady Capehart would not want to visit the nation's capital and not see where its laws are promulgated. Then we shall go on to Buckingham Palace."

James sighed. "Why not throw in Carlton House while we are about it?"

"I should love to see Carlton House!" Emma said.

James gave her a weary look. "Very well. Let us finish all the boring bits while we are here and have it over with once and for all. At least we can pass through St. James's Park on our way to the palace."

"It's rather far for the ladies to walk. We shall drive," Sanichton said.

Hansard noticed that Emma was disappointed at missing out on the park. When he had a private moment with Sanichton, he mentioned that perhaps they were tiring the ladies with so much viewing of grandiose architecture and suggested that they finish the tour for that day after viewing the Houses of Parliament. "What do you think, Lady Margaret?" he asked his companion.

"Whatever the rest of you want," Lady Margaret replied.

Sanichton agreed at once that the ladies were fagged. He had found Emma charming. Her enthusiasm reminded him of his own first trip to London and allowed him to feel sophisticated and experienced. His only regret was that Lord James was along to spoil the outing. They returned to Berkeley Square for tea. It was there that Sanichton said he would have a rout party the next evening in honor of Lady Capehart's first visit to London.

102

"What do you say, Maggie?" he asked his sister.

Lady Margaret looked to Hansard. "Does that suit your plans, Hansard?"

"A delightful idea! It's very kind of you," he said.

Lady Margaret, who not only approved of Lady Capehart for her brother but had an eye on Hansard herself, then felt free to approve the notion and became quite excited about it.

That evening James mysteriously disappeared immediately after dinner. Lord Hansard and Lord Sanichton took the ladies to a private musical evening at Lady Mayhew's and for supper at the Pulteney after. Miss Foxworth, who had spent an agreeable afternoon driving in a carriage with Lady Gertrude, was fagged. She remained at home with her hostess, discussing the exorbitant price of muslin and the solace to be found in novels. They were just retiring when Hansard brought Emma home. They said good night and went upstairs, the two gray heads nodding wisely over the ingenuity of Mrs. Radcliffe.

Hansard poured himself and Emma a glass of wine and settled in for a chat. "Well, how do you like London so far?" he asked her.

"It is precisely as I imagined, only better," she said. Her eyelids were already sliding closed, but she smiled in satisfaction. She looked like a tired child who was so enjoying herself that she didn't want to go to bed. "So many magnificent things to see. And we haven't even been to any parties yet."

"What do you think of Sanichton?"

"Oh, he is very nice," she said, but she didn't say it with the sort of enthusiasm Nick had expected. "A very sensible gentleman. He seems to know a great deal about everything. About cathedrals and historical things, I mean."

"He is very well to grass, you know. A fine estate and a mansion in London. You'll see the latter tomorrow evening at the rout party."

"Is he a good dancer?" she asked, stifling a yawn.

"Yes, excellent."

"That's nice, for I promised him the waltzes. James won't like it."

Hansard frowned. It was not so much at missing the waltzes as that mention of James. He gave her a wary glance. "Does it trouble you what James will think?"

"You're wondering if I still find your cousin fascinating, I expect. He is not much interested in serious things. He seems trivial beside Sanichton, yet Sanichton is almost too serious to suit me." She drew a weary sigh. "It really is difficult to find the right husband. I expect you experience the same thing in looking for a wife, Nick, or you would be shackled by now. Or have you discovered one who suits you?" she asked, and gave him a questioning look.

He again felt that heat rising around his ears. Was she going to repeat her proposal? James too trivial, Sanichton too serious—and himself in the middle, just right? He felt no sensation of anger on this occasion, but a surging excitement. What should he say if she proposed again? His impression of Emma had altered since that first proposal. He found her more interesting, more agreeable.

"What—what do you mean, Emma?" he asked, in a queerly choked voice.

"I am referring to Lady Margaret, of course. She's very nice. She suits you."

The excitement subsided, to be replaced by a definite sensation of pique. He had always found Lady Margaret too stuffy, too serious to please him—and not at all pretty. She was a fine lady of impeccable manners and sterling character, but not the sort to make a man's pulse quicken. In fact, she was cut from the same bolt as her brother. What had made him think Sanichton would do for Emma? She needed a livelier gentleman. Someone who would not prose her ear off with history lessons.

"We're friends, nothing more," he said stiffly.

"She likes you," Emma said. "Have you not noticed how she hangs on your every word and agrees with everything you say? Take care, Nick, or you'll receive another proposal. No, you shan't though. Lady Margaret would never be so indiscreet. She will only sit and wait and hope. You shouldn't encourage her if you don't mean to have her."

"I have never encouraged her in the least!"

"My mistake," she said, frowning. It was the same mistake she had made earlier, thinking Nick's friendly thoughtfulness indicated a deeper, more personal interest in herself.

"Where did you get such a notion?" he asked.

"I daresay it's simply that you're such a thoughtful escort. So nice," she added, regarding him fondly. "I'm grateful to you for saving me from a dreadful mistake."

"You would soon have discovered that Hunter was not for you without my help."

"Oh, but I didn't mean Hunter."

"About Lord James—"

She gave him a mischievous smile. "I didn't mean him either, Nick. Now who else could I have meant, I wonder? Why, William Bounty, to be sure."

Nick shook his head ruefully. Of course, she was referring to the infamous proposal. Would it have been such a dreadful mistake for him to marry Emma? At that moment, with the lamplight making a halo of her curls and her face pale after her late night, he felt an

105

urge to protect her, to cradle her in his arms and keep her safe. He made no reply. The room was quiet, save for the snap of logs burning in the grate, but it was a friendly, familiar silence.

"What was it that disgusted you so at my offer, Nick?" she asked. "I realize now that it was farouche of me, but the way you answered, so outraged. 'Marry *you*!' you said, as though I were a light-skirt or a—I don't know what. A yahoo. I wished I could have fallen through the floor. Yet you apparently think me good enough for your friend, Lord Sanichton."

Again Nick felt that heat around his ears. "I expect it was just the shock of it," he said. "I wasn't expecting anything of the sort. I'm sorry if I offended you. I ought to have laughed and made light of it. Blame it on my inexperience."

Why, he wondered, *had* he reacted so sharply, in a fashion that not only offended propriety but also wounded Emma deeply? Was it his demmed pride, thinking a provincial lass not good enough for him? Strange, when in well over a decade on the Town he hadn't met a single lady of the ton to attract him. They were either too obviously after the title or too jaded to appeal to him. He had thought that Emma was after the title as well, but her continuing interest in James didn't indicate a climber. He was only a younger son.

"I hadn't thought you would be inexperienced at anything," she said, again stifling a yawn.

Nick, on the other hand, was wide awake. That Emma could speak so openly about that encounter told him it held no particular significance for her. She had relegated it in her mind to a minor embarrassment. With Nick the thing seemed to grow in importance with the passing of time. It was taking on the significance of a turning point in his mind,

106

like a man reaching his majority or leaving university. He found himself placing recent occurrences in the context of her proposal. Things happened the day before or two days after the evening Emma Capehart proposed to him.

"That experience was entirely new to me," he said.

"And extremely unpleasant, I think. I hope you have no repetitions of it. And now I must retire." She rose and stood a moment, uncertainly, wondering how to take her leave of him. "Thank you for everything, Nick. It's been a lovely visit so far. Good night."

He rose and bowed. "Good night, Emma."

He sat on after she left, sipping his wine and thinking of ways to make the visit pleasant for Emma. Perhaps Sanichton had been a mistake. The gent he ought to have put forward, of course, was Lord Ravencroft. Why hadn't he? Again that niggling discomfort bedeviled him. She would love Ravencroft. All the ladies were running mad for him. And with his looks and charm, he was not the least debauched. Yes, he really ought to call on Ravencroft, but there was no hurry. Then he remembered that Emma had promised the waltzes to Sanichton and felt a stab of annoyance.

He worried, too, about having put ideas in Lady Margaret's head. It was true she always agreed with everything he said, but he had never taken it as a sign of attraction, only as feminine submissiveness. Actually, it annoyed him. He liked a lady who had a mind of her own and the courage to express it—like Emma.

For some time he sat on, filling his glass again and thinking. Was Ravencroft not just a little too fast for Emma? No, Emma would keep him in line. She could keep a lion or tiger in its place. They would make a marvelously handsome couple. Yet he disliked to think of Emma with Ravencroft. Something about it was just not right. Among other things, Ravencroft would make it so that he'd never have the waltzes with her again. He had always looked forward to them. She wouldn't come to him with her problems. But that was what he wanted—wasn't it, to be rid of her? He felt a little pang of loss to envisage a future without Emma to annoy him.

Chapter Thirteen

Lord James took Emma riding in Rotten Row the next morning as planned. Lady Margaret was very happy to let her new friend borrow her mount when it was learned that Lord Hansard was not riding. Hansard called on Sanichton and his sister regarding plans for the rout party that evening. He kept alert to discover whether Emma was right in her suspicion that Lady Margaret had a *tendre* for him.

Soon he was convinced it was true. The signs were subtle, but they were undeniably there. It was something in the way Lady Margaret looked at him, with soft smiles and frequent questions for his opinion, and her constant agreement with his every suggestion.

"We thought four musicians enough for a simple rout party. Did you like the fellows who played for Miss Berry's do?"

"Yes, excellent," he said.

"Then we shall have them. And I thought orgeat for your aunt and Miss Foxworth. . . . Does Miss Foxworth like orgeat?"

"I expect so. I know Aunt Gertrude does."

"I shall have some orgeat. About the music, Hansard, Horatio tells me Lady Capehart likes the waltz."

"Some waltzes would be nice."

"I, too, like the waltz," she said, smiling and waiting for the expected request.

Hansard dutifully asked her for the waltzes, and she accepted eagerly. Oh yes, Lady Margaret certainly had him in her eye. It was sharp of Emma to have seen it. He would have to dampen Margaret's enthusiasm before it got out of hand. Their being apart for the summer would do it. In the autumn he would lengthen his distance from Sanichton and his sister.

With all this on his mind, Hansard was already in an uncertain temper when he returned to Berkeley Square. His mood did not improve when the hour for James and Emma's return passed with no sign of them.

"They have lit out for Gretna Green, depend upon it!" Lady Gertrude exclaimed in delight. "James hinted as much the day they arrived."

"They were mounted. They would hardly head off to Scotland on horseback," Hansard said.

"A ruse to allay our suspicions until they are well beyond reach," Miss Foxworth pointed out. "They would hire a rig some place outside of London to throw us off the scent."

When Hansard remembered his chat with Emma the evening before, he couldn't believe she had eloped. Why would she? She was her own guardian. John had not placed any man in charge of her, no doubt thinking her papa more than adequate for the role. Was Emma so sly she had conducted that conversation to deflect suspicion of her scheme?

He called for his mount and pelted to Rotten Row, to discover if they had even been there at all. He arrived just as Bow Street was about to lead the pair of miscreants off to charge them with public mischief. The joyful lifting of his heart at seeing that

110

Emma had not eloped lessened his wrath at her imminent arrest.

And when Emma turned a grateful smile on him and cried, "Hansard! Thank God you have come!" what little anger he had managed to muster dwindled to something akin to amusement.

"What seems to be the problem, Officer?" he asked.

The officer tipped his hat in recognition of a leader of the ton. "Your lordship. Lord James and his young lady have caused a public mischief by galloping in Rotten Row and upsetting the old Duchess of Dearne. Her nag bolted on her, causing Her Grace to slide to the ground."

"It's soft falling. She didn't hurt herself," James said dismissingly.

"You know perfectly well the pace is kept to a walk in Rotten Row," Hansard scolded.

"And so I told him, your lordship," the officer threw in.

"Emma didn't know it," James said. "When she struck up a canter, I had to overtake her."

"Why didn't you tell her before you began your ride?" Nick asked.

"I thought she knew. Everyone knows. I'm surprised you or Sanichton didn't tell her."

"How is Her Grace?" Nick asked the officer.

"She cut up pretty stiff, which is why I felt I ought to take Lord James into custody. If you can straighten it out with her, I'll be glad to give up my commission on the arrest and let it pass." He looked hopefully to see if his lordship was of a mind to provide compensation.

A golden coin was passed between them. "Lady Capehart will write an apology to Her Grace," he said.

A much-chastened Lady Capehart followed Hansard out of the park at a strict walk.

"I'm sorry, Nick. I had no idea one could only

111

walk. What is the point of that? There is no exercise in walking your mount."

"The point is to see and be seen," James told her. "I wanted to show you off to the ton. I said I would make you famous, Emma. By nightfall your name will be known to everyone."

Emma cast a wary glance at Nick and was greatly relieved to see he was trying not to laugh. Served the demmed duchess right! The toplofty lady had snubbed a country cousin of Nick's the Season just past. A word by her whispered in Princess Esterhazy's ear had ruined another friend's hope of getting into Almack's. And worst of all, she was a Whig. Nick felt obliged to ring a peel over the pair during lunch, but they both knew his heart wasn't in it. Immediately after lunch the note of apology was written and dispatched, along with a bouquet of flowers.

Nothing was said of the contretemps when Lady Margaret called in the afternoon to take Lady Capehart shopping. During a delightful forage at the shops, Emma purchased new kid gloves, three pairs of silk stockings in various shades unobtainable in the country, a handsome new reticule, and a shawl for Miss Foxworth. Then it was back to Berkeley Square for dinner and to prepare for the rout party.

James had no intention of missing this do. He had rigged himself out in the height of fashion in a cinnamon jacket that well suited his complexion. The tumble of lace at his throat held a brown diamond the same shade as his eyes. His bow, when Emma came downstairs, was a model of exquisite grace.

He lifted Emma's fingers to his lips and exclaimed, "You put Aphrodite herself to the blush, Emma."

Emma thought she looked well in a gown of cream-colored Italian crape, gathered up around the hem with silk rosebuds. Other buds were tucked in among her raven curls.

"This is my London debut," she said. "I must look my best."

"Your worst would be better than any other lady there," he said gallantly.

But for all James's airs and graces and flattery, Emma found herself preferring Hansard's style. His modest jacket of dark green velvet clung to a set of broad shoulders. An equally modest emerald gleamed in his cravat. No fall of lace was considered necessary for a simple rout party.

"You look very nice, Emma," he said. His smile was the better compliment. A glow of pleasure lit his dark eyes.

As they drove to Sanichton's mansion, he mentioned some of the guests who would be there to meet her. "Tip of the ton," he said. "I tremble to mention it, but er—country manners won't do here. You and I are accustomed to speaking our minds. As you are especially interested in being at home in both societies, I shall mention only that discretion is the better choice amongst new acquaintances."

"I shall try not to disgrace you, Nick. I appreciate all the trouble you've taken on my behalf."

James emitted an occasional "Bah!" to show his disgust with the conversation.

Sanichton's mansion on Manchester Square was as grand as Nick had promised—and as imposing and lacking in welcome as a government building. Emma caught Nick's eye studying her as he pointed it out.

"Very impressive," she said, but there was no admiration in her voice.

James, on the *qui vive* for treachery, declared,

"It's only brick and stones and wood. True love is happy in a hut."

"Only until the snow flies," Emma said.

Their host welcomed them into a vast hallway done in carved oak and brown marble. Emma wondered why it was so gloomy for there was no lack of lamps. He introduced Emma with a very proprietary air to the other guests who had come before them. The guests were all from the cream of Society. There was hardly one amongst them who lacked a title. There was even a duke, fortunately not the husband of the Duchess of Dearne. Emma was aware of watchful eyes and raised eyebrows as Sanichton's friends examined her.

She found her tongue cleaving to the roof of her mouth, not knowing what to say, but Sanichton filled any embarrassing pauses until she recovered her social feet. Once she discovered it was not herself these people were interested in but the estate her late husband had left her, she could relax. They were suitably impressed with Whitehern, and if she had been a hurly-burly girl, they would have found no objection to her.

James was indignant when he discovered that Sanichton had got in first for the waltzes. "In that case, you shall have the first set with me, Emma," he declared, in such an aggrieved tone that she was not of a mind to dispute it.

He was very poor company as he whined and complained like a boy throughout the cotillion. "I took it for granted the waltzes were mine," he said. "I hadn't thought it necessary to make application for them like a stranger, after all we have been to each other."

"We've only known each other a week, James. There is no understanding between us."

114

"Sanichton has got at you with his title and gold. I'm disappointed in you, Emma."

"Yet you came to Whitehern to court me because of my gold."

"That was different. I'm only a younger son."

"Isn't it time you grew up?" she suggested.

"They've ruined you. You're no longer the free spirit I fell in love with. I shouldn't be a bit surprised to see you donning a court gown and making your curtsy come spring."

"A fate worse than death."

"If only you meant it!" he said with a kindling eye.

The waltzes with Sanichton were more enjoyable, yet they lacked that carefree spirit of her waltzes with James, or even Nick. He kept time to the music, he didn't step on her toes, but the dance never took flight.

"You have charmed the cream of Society, Lady Capehart," he complimented.

"I called the duke 'milord,'" she confessed. "He sounded very haughty when he told me a duke is called 'Your Grace.' Such an odd name for that graceless ogre. He looks like a gargoyle."

"The title is a compliment to his position in Society, not his physical appearance. He was more favorably impressed with your appearance. His Grace noticed a physical resemblance to Lady Hamilton. Only a physical resemblance, of course. She is counted a great beauty, you must know. We shan't mention her character in the same breath as yours. Imprisoned for debt, due to her own extravagance. Wretched woman! Hansard has assured me of your sterling character."

Emma was fully alive to the subtle condescension in his compliments. She had heard Nick protest at the harsh treatment accorded to Lady Hamilton. She could hardly come to cuffs with her host, however, so she smiled dutifully.

"And is His Grace a connoisseur of beauty?" she asked playfully, for there were rumors in that direction.

"Yes, by Jove! He has the prettiest—but I ought not to speak of that."

"I'm a widow, milord, not a deb. You may speak quite openly to me about worldly matters."

"Well, *entre nous*," he said uncertainly, "no secret after all, His Grace likes the ladies. But he is discreet, mind. He would never embarrass the duchess. A fine gentleman."

It was a relief when the waltzes were finished. Emma felt her face becoming tired from smiling when she wanted to raise her voice and complain. Had it not been for her duty to Nick, she would have spoken more openly to her host.

A smile of genuine pleasure lit her face when she saw Nick coming forward to rescue her. He had watched the progress of Emma's waltz with some trepidation. He knew her well enough to know that her tight smile often presaged some outrageous speech.

"Shall I take you outside for a good scream?" he asked, taking her elbow and leading her out of the ballroom.

"Was I that obvious?" she asked, laughing.

"I recognize the signs of frustration. What happened?"

She gave him a quick résumé of her disgrace with the duke and conversation with Sanichton. "I fear your friend is a tad high in the instep for me," she said.

"I expect you're right, but he's a good fellow, you know. Just the usual prejudices of his class."

"But you don't despise Lady Hamilton, and you're of the same class."

"She was younger and less experienced in worldly matters than Admiral Nelson. My own feeling is that *he* ought to have known better. Actually, it's usually the ladies who despise Lady Hamilton as a wrecker of marriage. Sanichton was probably trying to please you by denigrating her."

"I always prefer honesty in my dealings. If anything is to come of this match you are hatching, I shall have to give Sanichton a clearer view of how I feel about things."

Hansard looked at her in alarm. "Then you are serious about him?"

"He's handsome, rich, titled, and of good character. One cannot dismiss such a match out of hand."

"Quite," Nick said uncertainly. He had handpicked Sanichton and was hard put to now find a fault in him. "You would certainly want him to know your prejudices don't match his," he added. "What, exactly, did you have in mind?"

"His hypocrisy. He complains of Lady Hamilton for carrying on when she was married. Well, it was wrong of her, yet he praises the duke for his discretion in a similar matter. Surely the more important point is not the lack of discretion, but the wrongdoing in the first place."

"Society feels differently, Emma," Nick said simply. "The duke's marriage was arranged by his papa. Where there's marriage without love, there will be love without marriage."

"I'm familiar with that cynical bit of French philosophy," she said. "I disagree with it, as I disagree with the French on many other matters, like executing their monarchs and eating frog legs. People oughtn't to be forced into marriage if they're not in love, but if they do marry, then they should obey the vows they take before God."

Nick wondered if her papa had pressured her into marrying John. He said, "I fancy you and Sanichton would agree about the French at least. He is a firm royalist."

She listened with interest. "Actually, it might be interesting to sound him out on that other matter on which we disagree. I rather enjoy a good argument. But I don't have to tell *you* that. You have been my sparring partner long enough to know my horrid ways."

After a half hour of Lady Margaret's cloyingly agreeable company, Nick was ready for some friendly squabbling.

"You seem to have put our James in a pelter as well," he mentioned, handing her a glass of wine.

"I fear he is turning against me. He shook his head sadly and prophesied my ruin if I don't watch my step. He said I would end up making my curtsy at St. James's."

"Make sure he's not along, if you do. Queen Charlotte has taken him in dislike since he helped himself to a pinch of her snuff. One does not dip into the royal snuffbox without invitation. I haven't seen him since the first dance, by the by. Where is he?"

"Haring off after actresses, I expect. He looked as if he'd been at it all night when he turned up for breakfast this morning. At least he makes no bones about it. He admits he's a rakehell."

Again Hansard's lips moved. "I recommend you limit such country talk to the country, Emma."

She blinked in surprise. "I thought I was being uncommonly discreet! I was careful not to say *what* he had been at all night. At least there would be no

118

danger of Sanichton cutting up like that." She peered up at Nick. "Would there? He is not a secret lecher, is he?"

"No, no," Hansard said at once. "I wouldn't have introduced you to such a character."

She gave him a sly look. "Unless he happened to be a cousin and in need of a fortune."

"I had no idea James was such a wretch. We were discussing Sanichton. He is aboveboard in that respect."

Emma listened and thought for a moment before speaking. "He has asked me out to drive tomorrow. I shall give him some notion of my true feelings at that time. If he is too weak-stomached for my views, then I shall drop him. Or more likely he will drop me," she added.

"How do you plan to shock him?" Nick asked.

"I expect a word against the duke should do it. Just how lascivious is His Grace?"

Nick didn't hesitate a moment before giving her details. "He was lascivious to the extent of a five-thousand-pound set of diamonds for Lizzie Malton before giving her her congé and taking up with her younger sister. Lizzie was getting too old for him—she was nineteen."

"But he's ancient! He must be at least fifty."

"He prefers younger ladies."

"And Lord Sanichton called him a fine gentleman!"

"Well, the duke always votes the Tory ticket."

Nick felt a warm glow when he saw that wicked gleam in Emma's eyes. He felt the affair with Sanichton was about to come to a halt. James was pretty well past history. His conscience was easy on the matter of Lord Ravencroft. He had discovered that Ravencroft had left London.

119

"We haven't had our dance, Emma," he said. "Shall we?"

"Yes, it will be nice to stand up with someone I can talk to without walking on eggs," she said, setting aside her glass and taking his arm.

Chapter Fourteen

That morning Emma received a letter from her papa, forwarded by Derek from Whitehern. She read it with a sinking heart. He suggested that she hire a cottage by the sea for the summer. This would serve the double purpose of aiding Hildegarde's health, while removing Emma from the hammer blows on the roof of her home. As an extra bonus, he invited himself along for the sojourn. He enclosed half a dozen advertisements for cottages, each numbered in order of preference. Emma read the letter twice, then put it in her reticule, where it skulked like an ogre, threatening her happiness.

As luck would have it, Lord James was at home that morning when Sanichton came to call. James had decided that the proper treatment to bring Emma to heel was a frosty silence. That his left eye was swollen and discolored detracted somewhat from his dignity. No one asked how he had acquired the black eye. It was assumed that the actress's husband had shown up inopportunely the night before.

"Ah, Sanichton," James said, smiling grimly. "Taking Emma to look at more churches? I recommend Lambeth Palace. Perhaps the archbishop of Canterbury will invite you to tea."

"Actually, we'll be driving through Hyde Park," Sanichton replied.

James's young face colored alarmingly. "But that is *our* place, Emma!" he exclaimed. Then he leapt to his feet and left the room, muttering dire words of betrayal and treachery. From his limping gait, Emma assumed the blows last night had fallen on more than his face.

She was embarrassed, but Hansard just smiled vaguely. "James is always excitable as quarter day approaches," he said. "Enjoy your drive, folks."

After seeing them off, Hansard went to his study and tried not to think of Emma, driving out with Sanichton. What if Sanichton proved to have a sense of humor? What if he took Emma's scolding about hypocrisy in good form? It might be all that was needed to nudge her into accepting him. After half an hour Hansard began glancing at his watch. At the end of one hour he was at the saloon window, watching out for their return. After ninety minutes he convinced himself Sanichton had overturned his rig and called for his own carriage to go after them.

Before it arrived Emma came storming into the saloon, wearing a heavy scowl. Nick's heart lifted. He swallowed a grin and asked, "How did it go?"

"Wretchedly!"

"Gave him a good bear garden jaw for his hypocrisy, did you?"

She threw herself gracelessly onto a sofa. "Yes, and he forgave me! He blamed it on my innocence and was impressed at my high morals. He thinks ladies should be blind and stupid. Nick, I have the most horrid feeling that he is going to propose." She turned a tragic face on him. "What shall I do?"

He sat beside her. "If you don't care for him, then you must refuse."

She frowned as she drew off her gloves. "He'll write to Papa and ask permission. I know he will.

122

He's the sort who would do things properly. And he is really an excellent *parti*, you know. I can hardly hope to do better. Papa would approve of him. What excuse could I make for refusing? I had a letter from Papa this very morning." She mentioned the scheme of removing to a seaside cottage. "There is no point talking up a smallpox scare. He sent six advertisements, all for different parts of the coast." She drew a deep sigh and, after a moment, said, "I daresay I could manage Sanichton. One senses that sort of thing. Perhaps it would do after all."

"It was your scolding him for his hypocrisy that led to the bizarre notion you're a saint. You are hardly innocent of all wrongdoing, Emma. Give him a preview of your true nature. There is the matter of misleading your papa regarding Hildegarde's proposed visit to Whitehern, for example. I wager that subject didn't arise?"

"Indeed it did! I told him all about it when he began praising my innocence. I fear you got dragged into it," she said, biting her bottom lip and glancing uncertainly at Nick.

"I?"

"He took the notion you had put me up to it. What he actually said was, 'I would not have thought it of Hansard, leading a young girl astray. You would never be so underhanded, Lady Capehart. I shall ring a peel over Hansard.' I'm terribly sorry that you got dragged into it, Nick. I told him it was no such thing and begged him not to speak of it to you. Then he decided I was loyal to a fault. I hope you aren't very angry?" she asked in a small voice.

Nick was so far from being angry that he laughed aloud. "I shall soon set him straight if he broaches the matter to me."

"He won't believe you. He's putting me on a

pedestal, blaming my wretched faults on everyone else except me, as John did. That can only mean he loves me," she said, in a voice of doom.

The butler came to announce that Lord Hansard's carriage had arrived.

"Send it back. I shan't be needing it," Nick said.

Emma immediately apologized. "You're going out. Do go ahead. Don't let me detain you with my stupid problems."

"It wasn't important. This business of Sanichton is. We must devise a scheme."

She looked with interest to hear what he had in mind. "A plan to make him dislike me, you mean, so he doesn't write to Papa?"

"Exactly. As Sanichton has already tarred me with deceit, I have no compunction in abetting you."

"What do you suggest?"

After a frowning pause and a few turns up and down the room, he lifted his right hand and announced, "A masquerade party! Sanichton despises them. He dropped Miss Englehart when he learned she had attended the Pantheon masquerade. We shall have a masquerade party here at your insistence. I shall be against it, but you shall force me to it, buckle and thong, as only you can, my sweet shrew."

An impish grin seized her features. "Lovely! I really would love a masquerade. But would it be terribly infra dig, Nick? I don't want to give your friends a disgust of you, if it is not the thing."

"I wouldn't do it if it were 'not the thing.' It is only Sanichton's notion of debauchery. He fears folks will take advantage of their disguises to do things they shouldn't."

"Typical thinking of a hypocrite. Of course, we must invite him and Lady Margaret."

"Naturally. When he refuses you pout in your

adorable way and tell him if you and he have such different ideas of what is enjoyable, then there is no point in continuing to see each other."

"It would put you to a great deal of bother," she pointed out. "You must let me help defray the expense."

"The expense will be minimal, and Aunt Gertrude and Miss Foxworth can attend to the preparations—the invitations, and so on."

"It's very kind of you," she said, overwhelmed at his cooperation, especially as it was all in aid of turning off the suitor he had chosen for her. "I never meant to saddle you with so much bother when I proposed to you. I daresay you would like Sanichton very well for a neighbor, too, and are only doing this to help me."

"You've become an entirely troublesome wench," he said, smiling to soften his words. "It seems it would have been easier for me if I had accepted your first offer."

"Easier for the nonce," she said, "but only think of the long run—shackled to the troublesome wench till death did us part."

His lips opened in a slow, bemused smile. "At the rate you career along, death would not have been far away," he murmured. When Emma subjected him to a long, close scrutiny, for the tone did not match the words, he made an involuntary motion toward her.

Emma noticed a new look in his eye. She sensed some new feeling in the air, a charged atmosphere that made her uncomfortably excited, as if the blood had all rushed to her head. She changed the subject abruptly. "Now, about the party."

Nick shook himself back to attention. What was he thinking of? It would be ungentlemanly to strike up a flirtation with Emma when he had no intention of offering for her. She was a damnably attractive wench, but she had proved her ineligibility half a dozen times since reaching London. She didn't know how to address the ton, she galloped in Rotten Row—she didn't even know Romeo and Juliet died! In fact, it was deuced odd that a fellow so high in the instep as Sanichton was interested in her. The thought of Sanichton caused an angry wince.

"You must go in the disguise of some fairly risqué historical character, to make clear to Sanichton you're no better than you should be," he said.

"Salome, perhaps?" she suggested. "Though I don't know quite what one would wear. Diaphanous veils, I daresay. Or perhaps Mary Magdalene. She was no better than she should be. I've seen pictures of her. She usually wears scarlet."

He blinked. "Stop! I didn't mean quite that risqué! Next you will be saying Lady Godiva, to save the bother of any costume at all."

"No, my hair isn't long enough to play Godiva. It would leave me—exposed," she said, glancing down at her body.

Hansard felt a heat building up at her suggestions. "It is only Sanichton we hope to disgust, not the whole of Society."

"Are you suggesting my undraped body is disgusting?" she asked, bridling.

"I am hardly in a position to know, nor do I wish to discuss it. You will wear a costume. Perhaps go as Madame de Pompadour, in a French court gown and one of those high, powdered wigs." He studied her a moment, envisaging how she would look. Despite his best efforts she kept turning into Lady Godiva before his very eyes.

"A powdered wig? That sounds uncomfortable. How will you go, Nick?"

126

"As a mail-coach driver, in a red jacket with blue collar and cuffs, with a horn to clear the way. It was my ambition when I was a youth."

"Really? That's something you share with Derek, only he actually did it for a while. I would have thought you'd want to be prime minister."

"Oh no, I wasn't born old. I had my foolish dreams, once."

Lord James had become bored with his own company and joined them before Emma could follow up this interesting lead. James was so fascinated with the notion of a masquerade that he forgot he was sulking and entered wholeheartedly into the spirit of the thing.

"Emma shall go as Aphrodite, goddess of love!" he declared.

"Nick thinks I should go as Madame de Pompadour," Emma told him.

"A French harlot! Really, Emma. Have you no shame?" Nick bristled up at such loose talk in front of a lady, but James rattled on, unheeding. "You must be Aphrodite, so beautiful the wind lost its breath in admiration as she rose from the sea in the pearly mist of dawn."

"What sort of gown did she wear?" Emma asked.

"She rose from the waves au naturel. Don't explode, Cousin," he added aside to Nick. "Naturally we must portray her at a later date, after the three Graces had adorned her in clothes of shimmering hues, bejeweled, in a golden chariot pulled by doves."

"Poor doves," Emma said, laughing.

"Fortunate above all creation to be given the honor," he said, bowing. "And I, of course, shall go as Ares, god of war, her lover, in gleaming golden, plumed helmet, brandishing a sword. A warrior always works his way with the ladies."

"Why not as her husband?" Nick asked, curious.

"Because she didn't love Hephaestus. He was a hardworking bore. *You* might go as Hephaestus, Cousin," he added nonchalantly to Nick.

"I think not, thank you."

Emma blushed. He still resented her impetuous offer after all this time.

"The role of Ares particularly suits me," James continued, unaware of any discomfort in his listeners. "I have always felt an affinity with the poor, beleaguered fellow. His papa, Zeus, called him the worst of his children, just as Papa calls me. But the gods loved him. He survived and prospered. Yes, I shall go as Ares."

Nick turned to Emma. "And you, Emma?" he asked. "Will you go as de Pompadour?"

"No, I believe I shall go as Aphrodite," she said. "I cannot like to go as a French courtesan when I have been nagging at Sanichton about his friend's infidelity."

"Aphrodite was hardly innocent in that respect," Nick pointed out.

James said firmly, "It is settled, Cousin. Emma and I are going as Aphrodite and Ares. We shall be happy to arrange the details of the party for you. No doubt you have more serious matters to attend to—eh, Hephaestus?" he added slyly.

"As a matter of fact, I do. It is to be a smallish party, James. Don't go building an amphitheater in the ballroom."

James winced. "The amphitheater is of Roman origin, Cousin. Actually Etrusco-Campanian, but not Greek. I am not likely to make such an egregious error as that. A few Corinthian columns, strategically placed, with amphorae and marble busts on top,

128

will be sufficient to set the mood. You can hire them from Covent Garden for a pittance."

When Nick took a deep breath, Emma knew he was about to ring a peel over them and hastened to prevent it.

"The party hasn't a Grecian theme, James," she said. "It is only you and I who are dressing as Greek deities. I'm sure Nick's ballroom will do fine just as it is."

James thought a moment, then conceded that he had gotten carried away. "For me, there will be only the two of us at the party, but I take your point."

Emma went to speak to Hansard's aunt Gertrude. She and Miss Foxworth volunteered to write up the invitations. They settled on a date three days hence.

After Emma had left the saloon, James turned a questioning eye on his cousin. "You realize Sanichton will abhor the idea of a masquerade party, Cousin? It is the reason he turned off his last flirt. And to see Emma and me as lovers—he'll have uphill work keeping his jealousy on the leash. I shouldn't be surprised if he forgets himself and says *demme*."

"I realize it," Nick replied.

James's face melted into a winning smile. "You are the best of cousins. Do you know, I was beginning to take the absurd notion that you had changed your mind about me and Emma? I even accused you, in my heart, of trying to divert Emma's love from me by putting Sanichton forward. I have wronged you, Cuz. You were only exculpating my strange ways by exposing her to that consummate bore. You are throwing this masquerade to prevent his offering for my Emma."

"If you say so."

"Truth to tell, I was beginning to worry about Sanichton. Now that I know I have your approval, I shall repay you by mending my errant ways and proving an exemplary husband. My Ares days are over—except for the masquerade, of course. No more squabbling with Papa. I shall *settle down*," he said, adopting a noble mien, as if he were declaring his resignation to a heinous death.

Rising, he rubbed his blackened eye. "I feel like Mark Anthony after a gaudy night with Cleopatra." His motions, when he rose to leave, were unsteady. Nick figured the thrashing he had been subjected to had something to do with his promise of reformation. It wouldn't last, of course—but it might last long enough to fool Emma.

Nick's scheme to turn Sanichton off had borne strange and unwanted fruit. He could see, when Emma and James were together, that there was still a mutual attraction. They were both impetuous. They were apt to leap first and gauge the distance after. And she was eager to have someone to put forward to stave off her papa's visit. Had he just done something remarkably foolish?

Chapter Fifteen

The next day was spent making preparations for the masquerade party. The major arrangements were handled by the servants, of course. Emma, Hansard, and James planned a trip to the costumer in the morning to hire their outfits. Before they got away, Lord Sanichton's carriage arrived, and its extremely disturbed occupant came striding into Nick's saloon.

After bowing and greeting Emma, he said in a thin voice to Nick, "Might I see you in private a moment, Hansard?"

James, never one to keep his tongue between his teeth, asked mischievously, "Do let us all hear your complaint, Sanichton."

Sanichton stiffened and said, "Who said anything about a complaint?"

"Your chin said it, my dear fellow. When a man's chin takes to riding two inches higher than usual and his shoulders stiffen like concrete, he has either endured a thrashing or a complaint is forthcoming. Naturally you have done nothing to merit a thrashing," he said, making it sound like an insult.

Sanichton gave him a scalding look. "No doubt you would be familiar with complaints and thrashings, Lord James."

"Who better? It is Emma's masquerade party, I

expect, that has brought you pelting *ventre à terre* to cast aspersions on the innocent scheme?"

Sanichton glanced warily at Emma. "I did wish to have a word about it, as a matter of fact." As Hansard made no move to arrange privacy for the discussion, he took a seat and emptied his budget in front of them all. "Naturally you wish to entertain Lady Capehart during her visit, Hansard, but I really cannot think a masquerade party is the way to set about it. Lady Capehart would not realize the danger inherent in such carrying on."

Emma batted her long lashes and asked, "Whatever can you mean, milord? I particularly asked Nick if I might have one—when he mentioned having a little do for me, you know. I have always loved a masquerade party above anything."

Frustration consumed Lord Sanichton. The last thing he wanted was to deprive Emma of her treat, yet to see this innocent girl fall prey to the licentiousness of masked villains was more than he could tolerate.

"You are speaking of innocent country parties," he said. "In London, the masquerade has become an excuse for every wretched excess. Drunkeness, immodesty in dress, licentiousness. I should think you'd know better, Hansard."

"You may be sure that is not the sort of party that will occur under my roof," Nick said, mounting his high horse.

Lord James was even more irate. "Really, milord! You forget yourself. This is nothing else but an assault on Hansard's character to suggest he would permit anything of the sort. I don't know about you, Cousin," he said, turning to Nick, "but if anyone spoke so churlishly to me, I would call him out on the spot."

132

Sanichton saw that Nick was glaring at him, Emma was regarding him with distinct disfavor, and young James was bent on making mischief.

"Naturally I didn't mean Hansard would wittingly be party to such excesses," he said. "I hope you know me better than that, Hansard. It is the matter of wearing disguises that leads folks astray. Hide a man's face, and he feels free to give vent to his lowest cravings. And with an innocent little creature like Lady Capehart—"

"Ah, but you misunderstand the matter, Sanichton," Nick said smoothly. "I am inviting only ladies and gentlemen to the party, not a parcel of debauchees. I trust my friends can behave themselves, even with the upper half of their faces hidden."

"If you feel the temptation will prove too strong for you, Sanichton—" James said. Sanichton gave a *bah* of disgust. "A man of character will hardly turn into a wild beast only because he wears a mask," James added. "Only a craven coward would behave so."

Sanichton saw that he was being shown in a poor light. Emma was regarding him suspiciously, as if he might assault her, if he had the concealment of a mask.

"It's true it will be a small, private party, with only the cream of Society," he said, frowning and wringing his hands. "Not like a public brawl at the Pantheon. No doubt you've heard of the wretched excesses perpetrated there?"

"Not all that wretched," James said, with an air of authority. "I've seen more drunkards at the Duchess of Memme's balls. Or were you referring to the light-skirts, Sanichton?"

"There is no need to discuss this in front of Lady Capehart," he said stiffly. Then he turned to Nick. "If you can guarantee there will be no improper behavior, then Lady Margaret and I will be happy to attend."

Nick stared at him as if he were looking at some reprehensible lower form of life. "I am not in the habit of guaranteeing security for my guests. Surely that is taken for granted. If you feel the least concern for your safety, then naturally you must not put yourself out to attend. I accept your excuse for declining."

"It's not myself I'm worried about! It is Lady Capehart. And, of course, Margaret."

"Very considerate, Sanichton," Nick replied, his nostrils thinning, "but there's no need for you to concern yourself for the safety of a lady under my roof."

Sanichton realized his concern for Lady Capehart had led him into a grave social solecism. "Of course. I'm sorry I offended you, Hansard. Naturally you will take every precaution for Lady Capehart's safety. I don't know if you heard the tale, but it happens my cousin Miss Trueman was viciously assaulted at a masquerade party in Brighton by a drunken officer. A chap from an excellent family, too. My cousin, I fear, was not wholly innocent. She wore a somewhat revealing costume. Again, the masquerade was used as a pretext for immodesty. The matter was hushed up, but it has left me with a distaste for masked parties."

"If you feel that way, I don't think you should come," Emma said at once. "We would not want you to be uncomfortable all evening. We quite understand, don't we, Nick?"

"Oh, no! I shall come," Sanichton said. Emma stared at Nick with a stricken look on her face. Sanichton turned to her and asked in a conciliating tone, "And what costume have you chosen, Lady Capehart?"

134

"Emma will come as Aphrodite, and I as Ares," James announced. "We were just on our way to hire costumes when you arrived." He glanced impatiently at his watch.

"Don't let me detain you," Sanichton said. He was unhappy to think of Lady Capehart being made even more desirable by a revealing gown, but he didn't want to draw further wrath by hinting at his feelings. He could count on her and Hansard's discretion. Aphrodite wore various disguises after all. No doubt Lady Capehart would wear a modest evening gown, with, perhaps, her hair out loose. As he had no idea who Ares was, this didn't concern him.

"Hansard is going as a coach driver," Emma said. "How will you come, milord?"

"I hadn't given it any thought. I don't attend—*usually* don't attend masquerades."

"The wig and robes of a judge suggest themselves as suitable," James said with a sneer.

Sanichton looked interested. "There have been a few judges in my family. I shouldn't be surprised if we have the robes in the attic." He rose and began to take his leave. "You haven't forgotten Lady Margaret is escorting you to her modiste's establishment this afternoon, Lady Capehart?"

"I look forward to it," Emma said.

After Sanichton left James said, "Bad enough he is a prude, he hasn't even a sense of the ridiculous. Imagine not realizing I was roasting him about posing as a judge."

"We were rather hard on Sanichton," Emma said. "I felt wretched. I didn't realize his cousin had been assaulted at a masquerade."

"And the party didn't turn him off either," James said. "But it has weakened his determination to have you. I saw him blink when I told him you were to go as Aphrodite. Come, let us choose the most daring outfit in the shop to disgust him. Unfortunately, it will also arouse his wanton impulses. Any man who is so concerned for morality is trying to control his own wayward tendencies. I know that seeing you as Aphrodite will arouse mine. Perhaps even yours, eh, Cuz?" he added aside to Nick.

"Perhaps even mine, moribund though they be," Nick agreed.

"Missing Mrs. Pettigrew, are you?" James asked.

"Desperately."

Nick glanced at Emma, who was examining him curiously. She scowled. She remembered distinctly that Nick had claimed Mrs. Pettigrew was only a friend, yet surely James would know the true situation. And Nick had as well as confirmed it. She was aware of a sense of grievance that she had no right to. What was it to her if Nick had a mistress?

"Shall we go?" Nick said. "I hear the carriage."

Emma was still enough of a tourist to enjoy the trip through town. The plethora of handsome carriages rattling along, the dandies and ladies on the strut, the shop windows offering all manner of enticement were like magnets to her. James and Nick exchanged a speaking smile as she sat with her nose glued to the window, drinking in all the wonders of London.

"I'll take you on the strut after we hire our costumes," James said, and seized her fingers. Nick, watching, noticed that she didn't withdraw her hand.

Once they were in the costume shop, James became lost in imagination. The shop didn't have an outfit designed specifically for Ares, but they had gilt helmets with magnificent red plumes, shining breastplates, swords, and all manner of ancient military accoutrements. That he could hardly dance while carrying so much metal didn't seem to occur to him, and Nick certainly didn't mention it.

Nick found a coachman's outfit to fit him with no difficulty. It was a favored costume. Emma chose a white gown with a vaguely Grecian look to its draped style. James selected a diadem of glass stars for her head and a jeweled corset to wear around her waist. It pinched, but it looked well.

"Just look at the size of that waist, Hansard," he said in awe, when the costumer cinched the corset around her. "I could span it with my two hands. And it enhances the bosoms beautifully. We must watch her closely, or your friend Sanichton's dire foreboding might well come to pass. If only she were a blonde, she would be perfect."

"Surely Grecian ladies are more usually dark haired," Nick said. He had been admiring the sheen of Emma's lovely raven hair.

"Contemporary Grecian ladies, yes, but we are speaking of goddesses of antiquity. It is Botticelli's famous painting that has given us the notion Venus—the Roman interpretation of Aphrodite—was a blonde. Perhaps a wig . . ." He strolled off in search of a long blond wig.

"What do you think?" Emma asked Nick.

"I think Sanichton will probably propose," he said. "And I was so certain the party would be enough to disgust him."

Emma gave him a conning smile. "It seems he is more enamored of me than you realized."

"So it seems," Nick replied, displaying very little interest. "We are putting ourselves to a deal of bother for nothing."

"Not for nothing, surely. A masquerade is fun. Will you not enjoy it?"

He studied her for a long moment. "Perhaps—if you'll save me the waltzes. We've been missing our waltzes, Emma."

"I'm afraid Ares has got in before you," she said, casting a questioning look at James, who was strutting in front of a mirror.

"Do I sense a warming of your affections in that direction?" Nick asked.

"I never know quite what to make of James, but despite all, I prefer him to your sanctimonious friend, Sanichton."

Nick just smiled and went to help James in his selections. He suggested a set of metal shin and knee protectors that would make waltzing impossible. James strapped them on and wielded his sword.

"It is the true me," he said, striking a pose before the mirror. "I am that sort of fellow who can be either very good or very bad, but I cannot be mediocre. I shall make a superb Ares, lover of Aphrodite. I wish Papa would let me have my portrait done in this outfit. He is such a dead bore. He wants me to wear a hunting jacket and stand beside Warboy, his latest equine acquisition. He don't fool me! It is his hunter he wants a portrait of. I am merely the pretext. What do you think of this plume, Cuz? Does it wave gallantly when I turn my head?"

"Gallantly. But don't you think you need a longer sword? That one is hardly long enough to kill a mouse."

"True, but the hilt is magnificent. Still, you may be right . . . ."

He went in search of a longer sword, which would add another impediment to dancing. Hansard returned to Emma.

"James won't be able to dance, carrying so much metal about him," she said.

"No, but he will look magnificent," Nick replied blandly. "The show's the thing, you must know."

She looked at him wearily. "It isn't going to be a wretched party, is it? I mean with Sanichton scowling, and James acting up, and you—"

"Me?"

"All your time and effort for nought, if Sanichton offers."

"We shall have to see that he don't."

Her face firmed to determination. "Yes, I must behave rather badly, I fear. That should do it."

Nick drew a deep sigh. "And here you were worried that it would be a wretched party."

Chapter Sixteen

The days passed in a flurry of pleasure and excitement. Lady Margaret took Emma to her modiste that afternoon, where Emma succumbed to the temptation of a new gown and a new riding habit, the latter to be made up in the military style with epaulettes and brass buttons. In the intimacy of this ancient feminine pursuit, Margaret and Emma became better acquainted. Margaret sensed a free-spirited girl who strained at the shackles Sanichton imposed. She thought Emma would be good for her brother, who could be a prosy old bore if he wasn't prodded from time to time. She gave Sanichton a hint of her feelings when she returned, and he listened eagerly.

"She is a darling, isn't she?" he asked in a moonish way.

"Delightful," Lady Margaret agreed, "and very well to grass. I do hope you weren't too severe about the masquerade. Under Hansard's auspices, you know, it will be unexceptionable. What costume will you choose?"

"We have that judge's robe and wig in the attic. Lord James mentioned I might go as a judge."

"Oh, Horatio! Choose something more dashing, or you'll seem to be nothing but an old stick alongside the others. Lord James suggested it purposefully to make you look a quiz."

That evening Lady Margaret invited Emma, Hansard, and James to attend a rout party being given by her friend Miss Almonte. The company, unfortunately, inclined to dullness.

"They've ransacked the pews of the Methodist church to gather this lot," was James's indictment. "There's not a pretty face in the batch of them, except for Sir Hillary Dane."

Miss Almonte had invited only the most rigidly moral of her acquaintances. Emma found Sanichton relatively easygoing in comparison; he stood up with her for the waltzes.

"I hope you don't think me an old stick-in-the-mud about your masquerade party, Lady Capehart," he apologized. "It was only concern for your innocence that led me into that wretched indiscretion this morning. I could see Hansard was on his high horse. Truth to tell, it was not his party I was worried about so much as Lord James. A bit of a rascal, Lord James. Let him hide his face and there's no saying what he might get up to. Sly as well, suggesting I go as a judge. Maggie thinks he was quizzing me."

"How will you come to the party?" she asked to avoid this subject.

"In a manner that will shock you," he said, and laughed in a way he hadn't laughed before, as if he were enjoying himself.

"Now don't tease, Lord Sanichton. What is your costume?"

He gazed into her gleaming eyes. "Perhaps I shall come as Don Juan, or Romeo, or some fellow with an eye for the ladies."

Emma looked at him with the dawn of a new

interest. "You have been hiding your light under a bushel, Lord Sanichton."

"As Maggie was saying, you're not a deb after all, but a widow. I fear I have given you a poor notion of me with my carping." His arms tightened, drawing her closer to him, though not close enough to cause concern in the most demanding matron. "Now don't you think it time you stopped lording me?" he asked daringly.

"If you wish, Sanichton."

"I didn't mean that! My name is Horatio. I would be honored if you would call me so."

"Horatio," she said, thinking the stodgy name suited him.

"May I call you Emma?"

"Why not? Oh! Now I know how you will come to the party. You are going to be Horatio Nelson! He had an eye for the ladies, as we discussed the other evening."

"Yes, an eye for his own Emma. Only one eye, and only one arm to cuddle her as well," he said, soaring to unusual heights of recklessness. "Though I oughtn't to make jokes about his misfortune," he added, when Emma stared at the new personality that was peeping tentatively out from this stern moralist. "I had not planned to come as an admiral, however."

Emma teased him some more about his costume. He daringly mentioned the similarity of their first names, Emma and Horatio, to those of that famous couple, Lord Nelson and Lady Emma Hamilton, and hinted at his own similar feelings. Emma found, to her surprise, when the waltzes were over, that she had enjoyed them. She noticed, too, that Nick had had the waltzes with Lady Margaret, who was glowing like the sun in pleasure. The two couples walked toward each other, then continued together toward the refreshment parlor.

Once there Lady Margaret was accosted by Miss Almonte, and Sanichton immediately did the proper thing by requesting her to stand up with him. He took Emma's hand before leaving and said, "Pardon me, Emma. Duty calls."

Hansard's ears perked up at that casual "Emma." When Margaret was led off by a friend, Nick served Emma a glass of wine and drew her to the side of the room for some private conversation.

"I didn't see any sign of freezing in Sanichton when you were waltzing with him," he said.

"More like a thaw," Emma replied. "Really he is much more lenient in his views than I had thought. He even attempted a few jokes."

"I notice he's achieved a first-name basis as well. I fear the letter to your papa is imminent," he said, lifting an eyebrow.

"I shouldn't be at all surprised," she said, with something akin to complacence. That letter with the list of cottages was still in her reticule, awaiting a reply. Between the gay round of activities and uncertainty as to what to write, she had not answered it. If she could say she was engaged, the matter would be solved.

Nick stared at her. "Are you suggesting that, after all my efforts to deter him, you *welcome* his advances?"

She sighed. "I'm not sure, Nick. But really, when you think of it, most of your efforts were to bring us together. It's only the masquerade that was designed to turn him off, and it seems to have brought a new side of him to light, a more likable side."

"Well this is a fine how-do-you-do!"

"Now don't sulk," she said, patting his fingers. "If

143

I accept his offer—if he offers, I mean—then your job is done. You'll be free of your troublesome neighbor. I shall have Horatio to pester with all my little problems. Isn't it worth the bother of coming to London and having this masquerade party to be rid of me?"

"What of James?" he asked, and blushed at the folly of such a question.

"What about him? He'll find some new actress to fall in love with."

"Only this morning you were telling me your feelings for James had undergone a change. You were finding him more agreeable."

"So I was." She smiled impishly. "I'm really not at all hard to please, you see. Any gentleman will do for me."

"Then it's a pity we bothered coming to London," he said grouchily.

"Oh, but I meant any gentleman who knows his way about Town. William Bounty, for instance, would not have done at all. And Derek was only after my blunt. I think Horatio likes me for myself. I shall confess all my horrid little tricks about misleading Papa before I let him make an offer, however. It wouldn't be fair to him not to."

"You've already confessed that."

"Not all of my stunts. I've been staving off Papa and Aunt Hildegarde for months, you know."

"That won't be enough to deter him. He'll turn you into a tragic heroine, being forced into an unwanted match."

"They do say love is blind, but at least I shall have no secrets from him."

"You plan to accept him, then?" Nick asked, and held his breath for her answer. He knew he should be relieved. Sanichton was an excellent *parti*. He had chosen him himself. Emma couldn't be in better hands. Yet he was not pleased. Something bitter caught in his throat at the very thought of them together.

"I don't know," she said simply, and looked at him trustingly. "It's true James has been behaving more sanely recently. It is very difficult making the right match. It's especially important for a lady, you must know. She depends totally on her husband for her welfare. Is James likely to squander my estate?"

"I shouldn't be at all surprised," Nick said.

"Nor should I. When all is said and done, Sanichton is the better match. I shall watch him closely and see if he improves on longer acquaintance. And by the by, you are still leading Lady Margaret astray. She was glowing during the waltzes, Nick. What on earth were you saying to her?"

"We were discussing our costumes for the masquerade. She plans to come as a shepherdess. I told her she would make a charming shepherdess. Is that cause for a lady to glow?"

Emma considered it a moment before speaking. "That would depend on how you said it. Did you gaze into her eyes and murmur softly, or did you just glance over her shoulder and say it offhandedly?"

"I didn't murmur at all! I believe I looked at her. It is only common courtesy."

Emma nodded. "It would be the look that did it. I remember you used to look at me like that. To flatter John, I mean. I realize now you didn't mean anything by it. What a little fool I was. I actually thought you were in love with me."

Nick listened and tried to recall those early days of his acquaintance with Emma. He didn't remember trying to flatter John by flirting with his wife. He had been impressed by Emma's beauty. Perhaps he had let himself get a little carried away.

"Why are you looking like that?" she demanded.

"Like what?"

"Frowning, as if you don't remember. You know perfectly well you were a wicked flirt, so long as you knew I was safely married."

"I admit nothing of the sort!"

She gave a derisive look. "No doubt it, like everything else, is to be blamed on my naïveté. I misinterpreted your leers for flirtation."

"I never leered at a lady in my life!"

James came sauntering up to them. "What a dead bore you are, Cuz, never leering at a lady. I have worn my eyes out with leering. I've just been leering at Lady Margaret. She's looking well this evening. I do believe she has found herself a beau. Or perhaps she was trying to flirt with me."

"What did she say?" Emma asked, interested.

"She called me a wicked boy. All I did was pinch her. There is nothing so flattering as being called wicked by an older lady."

Nick gave a *bah* of disgust.

"Don't flatter yourself it's you she has in her eye. She is in love with Nick," Emma said. "She asked me a dozen questions about you this afternoon, Nick. The sort of subtle questions a lady asks when she's interested, but doesn't want to reveal it. She supposed your family must be eager to see you settled, and wondered about when you might be likely to oblige them, and that sort of thing."

"A fellow could do worse," James advised his cousin. "For a wife, I mean. Well to grass and not pretty enough to cause any scandal. Once she was settled in at Waterdown with a parcel of brats, you could enjoy your flirts during the Season in London."

Emma listened and began to think James was not

146

at all the sort of husband she wanted. Nick glanced at Emma and saw the disenchantment on her lively face.

"Very edifying, James," he said.

James looked aghast. "I didn't mean that was the way *I* would carry on! Good God! I only meant—As if Emma would be content to sit at home. Naturally you shall come with me to London every Season. I shall insist on it, my pet."

"Will you, Master Jackanapes? I doubt very much you will ever be in a position to insist upon anything, where *I* am concerned." She rose and flounced from the room.

"What a gauche thing for me to say," James exclaimed, crestfallen. "And just when things were going so well. I shall rush off and re-enchant her."

Nick sat on alone a few moments, pondering the muddle of romance. Then he recalled that he was to have the next set with Emma and went chasing after her. He found her in the ballroom, sitting in a corner, looking sullen. He joined her.

"Sit down. I'm hiding from James," she said. "I've come to a decision, Nick."

His heart clenched like a fist. Following her gaze, he noticed it was Sanichton she was looking at. She had decided to accept him, then. "I see," he replied, in a tolerably calm voice, considering the state of his emotions.

"Yes. I shall definitely not accept James. His character is too unsteady. He's a lecher, and he has no notion of giving up his ways after marriage. No one is perfect, of course. One must choose the lesser imperfection. I should prefer Sanichton's prudishness—and it will be easier to change," she added.

"So you have decided to accept Sanichton?"

"I didn't say that! I said I shall definitely *not*

accept James. I shall tell him so when we get home. It is only fair."

"Fair—but is it wise, when he's already arranged his Ares costume to match your Aphrodite?"

"You're afraid he'll make a scene?"

"I'm afraid he'll use the excuse of a broken heart to fall into some wretched hobble, while he is under my roof."

"He's already been carrying on with a light-skirt and had his eyes darkened by her husband. What worse can he do?"

"That is what I don't care to find out."

"I'll be gentle with him. He doesn't really love me, you know. He merely likes the idea of a lady who isn't terribly ugly or ill-natured and has a fortune besides."

"Who wouldn't?" Hansard asked, in a rhetorical spirit.

"I can think of one gent who didn't," she said, with a pert, meaningful smile. Then she rose and took his arm to join a set on the dance floor.

As they drove home after the party, Emma wondered what it was in her that Nick disliked. Her head reeled with compliments from the other gentlemen she had stood up with. Derek, James, and Sanichton had been smitten from first glance. She knew her fortune and estate were a part of her charm, but the estate should be of particular interest to Nick, as it marched with his own acres.

The feeling was growing in her that no other gentleman would suit her so well as Nick. He was good and kind and honorable without being strait-laced. She could talk to him freely without fearing he would either try to seduce her or read her a lecture. When she had proposed to him, she hadn't felt this way at all. She hadn't really cared what he thought of her then. He simply was a good *parti* and a good neighbor, who would have made a good-natured husband to keep Aunt Hildegarde at bay. Now she would no more propose to him than she'd go calling on the queen. She wished with all her heart that she had never made that foolish offer, for she felt that was at the root of her problem.

And to have said to a gentleman who needed an heir that she only meant a marriage of convenience on top of all the rest—why, he must think her a complete idiot!

Chapter Seventeen

Emma asked Hansard to leave her and James alone a moment when they reached Berkeley Square. "I want to get this over with, or I shan't sleep all night," she whispered.

"I'll be nearby, in case he turns violent."

Nick went to his office and waited, listening for the breaking of china and crashing of chairs that would indicate Emma had turned James off.

James, as was only to be expected, refused to take any blame for her decision. It was the fault of that prosy old bore, Sanichton; of Hansard for having presented the fossil to Emma; of Emma herself for being so easily swayed. When Nick heard the first crash, he went darting to the saloon, afraid the crockery might have been aimed at Emma.

"There is no need to carry on as if you were heart-broken, James," Emma said blandly. "You'll find another girl." She turned to Nick. "Sorry about the vase, Nick, but it was only that ugly old blue one from the mantle."

"I don't want another girl! I want you!" James cried.

Nick picked up the shattered remains of a Chinese ginger jar and dumped them in the grate.

"Next time you set out to con a lady, I suggest you behave yourself until you have the ring on her finger," Emma said. "Late hours and black eyes are not attractive, James."

James reached for a silver candlestick. Nick removed it from his fingers as he took aim at the mirror.

"Go out and get drunk," Nick suggested. "It's easier on the knickknacks. That was a valuable Chinese vase you destroyed."

"Papa will repay you," James said stiffly. "And who is to repay me for my suff—agony?"

"Rubbish. You're enjoying yourself thoroughly," Emma said. "The next best thing to pretending you're in love is pretending you have a broken heart."

"What would you know of love?" James asked grandly. "At least the gods will be happy. Plato tells us they enjoy a good joke." On this speech he stalked from the room.

"Well, it's done," Emma said. "Sorry about the vase, Nick. I shall replace it. His juvenile behavior makes me appreciate Horatio. I really am dreadfully sorry that this occurred in your home."

Nick poured two glasses of wine and handed Emma one. She sat down, and he sat beside her.

"It's I who should be apologizing. I had no idea James was such a fool when I sicced him on you. The family manages to keep his folly under wraps. It must be a full-time career for them."

"It was kind of you to try to find me a husband. It's the thought that counts. I hope you won't think it horrid of me, Nick, but after John's death—after the shock of it wore off, you know—I used to imagine what it would be like, being free to go about with other gentlemen. I never had any beaux at all before my marriage. I missed all that—romance," she said, tossing her hands vaguely. "I thought it would be so

lovely, but it's really difficult. It seems everyone
wants something from me. Not Sanichton! I'm not
disparaging him. You asked me before if I had
decided to have him, and I said I wasn't sure. Now
I'm sure. He's the best of the lot."

"I can't argue with that," Nick agreed. "But don't
you feel you're rushing things? You ought to give
yourself a Season."

She drew a deep sigh. "I should love it of all things,
but I don't have any relatives who could sponsor me.
I'm getting rather old to try to masquerade myself as
a deb, and besides, Papa would never sit still for it."

"I daresay Aunt Gertrude would act as your
sponsor, now that she's got her own daughter
launched. You're a little older than the debs, but
hardly hagged," he said, studying her youthful face.
He read the yearning in her eyes and the softly
curving lips, drawn into a half smile.

"You don't understand," she said, shaking her
head. "Papa would be on the doorstep within twenty-
four hours if he ever heard of such a thing. And there
would be no keeping it secret. The papers publish
lists of the ladies being presented. Aunt Hildegarde
simply devours all the court news. Papa thinks
London quite wicked, you must know. Besides, I'm
too provincial. I always say the wrong thing and do
the wrong thing. With Sanichton and Lady Margaret
to watch out for me, I shall do better."

Nick thought a lady about to accept an offer
should look happier. Emma wore a sad, resigned
face, like a child on her birthday who'd been
expecting a bright, new doll and had to settle for a
pair of stockings. He felt an odd twisting in his chest
that he ascribed to pity. He was quite sure of one
thing. Emma didn't love Sanichton. She was just
determined to marry. He felt sorry for her, and frus-

trated. It seemed hard that a young lady couldn't have even one real romance in her life. Emma might be a hoyden, but there was no vice in her. He had misjudged her.

Before he could reply, Emma said, "It's strange James hasn't left. I didn't hear the door slam, did you?"

"He went abovestairs."

"I wonder what he's up to."

Nick felt a frisson of alarm himself. "I'll find out," he said, and went darting upstairs. He returned in a few minutes. "He's gone to bed," he said.

"That's odd."

"He asked the butler for a sleeping draft."

"Good God! He's letting on he's committing suicide. He might take the wrong dose and kill himself."

"Simms gave him only a small dose, so we needn't fear he'll lumber us with a corpse."

"Then I suppose we might as well retire, too." Nick rose and gave her his hand to help her up. "Once again, I apologize, and thank you for all your help, Nick."

On an impulse she reached up and placed a light kiss on his cheek. The brush of her velvet-soft lips against his cheek set off a buzzing in his ears. A warmth grew within him, softening his insides until he felt weak. The delicate scent of a flowery perfume wafted over him—feminine, alluring. He took her hand and raised it to his lips. A warm kiss brushed her hand.

"Good night, Emma," he said softly. He watched as she walked away, with a gentle swaying of her hips. She wore her hair up that evening. Tendrils of raven curls had escaped to nestle against her ivory neck. He stood watching until she disappeared through the door. Then he raised his fingers and drew them slowly over his cheek, still warm from her kiss. He wore a puzzled frown, as if trying to figure out a difficult problem.

In the morning Lord James had resumed his modest clerical attire and manner. "Good morning Lady Gertrude, Miss Foxworth, et al," he said, bowing to the company assembled at the table. "Sorry I'm late. I slept poorly last night." A darkly accusing gaze swept over Emma, but he said no more.

"What are you up to today, James?" Lady Gertrude asked.

"I am calling on Dean Stanton, a friend of Papa's, to ask his opinion on a certain matter."

This was assumed to indicate he was about to resume his interrupted career. Emma, studying him, expected to see a faux-noble mien and was dismayed to discover a sly light in his eyes as he peered at her. Dean Stanton my eye, she said to herself. He's up to something.

She mentioned her fear to Nick, after the older ladies had left to raid Hatchard's in search of new novels.

"I noticed," Nick said. "I fancy he's trying to win you back by the role that originally attracted you—hardworking, noble cleric."

"He must think me a simpleton to fall for the same stunt twice."

"He doesn't suffer from any excess of brains. Is Sanichton calling for you this morning?"

"No, he mentioned some business at the House. Lady Margaret is taking me to call on her aunt this afternoon."

"Being vetted as the future Lady Sanichton, eh?" Nick asked, trying for a cheerful tone.

"I expect so," she said glumly.

Nick excused himself and had his curricle brought

around. He didn't believe for a minute that James was calling on Dean Stanton. The whelp had some trick up his sleeve, and he must scotch the plan. Nick was curious, but not entirely surprised, to see James's rig stop in front of Sanichton's house. Nick drove around the corner and returned to Manchester Square when he saw James's carriage leave. Had the pup issued a challenge to Sanichton? Nick was happy to learn from Margaret that her brother had already left for the House.

"Lord James wasn't calling on Sanichton," she said, smiling archly. "It was me he was calling on, actually. What a rogue he is! He asked me to save him the waltzes at your masquerade, Hansard."

"Did he mention Emma?"

"Yes, I told him we were going out this afternoon. He didn't offer to join us when he heard it was Lady Sefton we were to call on. She is on nettles to meet Horatio's lady. We all adore Lady Capehart," she added. "Such a treasure, and completely unspoiled. Not like the jaded ladies one meets in London."

Nick stayed chatting for fifteen minutes to see what else he could glean, then he left. It was unsettling to learn James was trying to discover where Emma was spending the day. He felt in his bones that James was bent on revenge, but a visit to Lady Sefton left little room for misbehavior.

When Nick returned a note from James awaited him. It said that he was taking lunch with Dean Stanton and would be there for most of the afternoon as they found they had so much to discuss. Since James hadn't called on Stanton, Nick knew his fears were well founded. He'd have to follow Emma when she went to call on Lady Sefton. He didn't envy Emma her afternoon. The dame was a formidable bastion of propriety.

Emma did indeed look wilted when she came out of the house, but of James there was no sign.

When Nick inquired later at Berkeley Square how the visit had gone, Emma said, "I passed muster. I could see Lady Sefton thought me gauche and provincial, but the estate won her over. She called me 'well behaved.'"

James continued his righteous ways over the next days, wearing his subdued vestments and sitting with a book of sermons propped up before him, while the others went about their business. Between Lady Margaret and Sanichton, Emma was kept hopping. Sanichton regaled her mornings with trips to the historical hot spots of London, an amazing number of which featured deaths and violence. The afternoons were more pleasant. Lady Margaret took her visiting and shopping.

Nick watched as the girl physically wilted, from either fatigue or boredom. He felt still that unsettling feeling that he ought to do more for Emma, but what more could he do? She had decided on Sanichton, and all he could do was help her.

He hadn't much time to think about it. James was behaving much too well to please him. Nor was he doing it to impress Emma. Emma, in her blunt way, had told him to stop behaving like a gudgeon and go out and enjoy himself, for he was not impressing her by acting like a minister and dressing like an undertaker.

"It will astonish you to learn, Lady Capehart, that I am no longer leading my life to suit you," James said nobly.

"You never were. If you think running about with the muslin company and getting into brawls suits me, you are very much mistaken."

James regarded her pale face with satisfaction.

"Odd that finding your true love has put you in such a black humor, Lady Capehart."

"It is you who puts me out of sorts. I wish you will not loaf about, pretending you're reading sermons. I know very well you have a book of poetry hiding under that black tome. The cover is peeping out."

When Nick discovered that it was the poetry of John Donne that was being read in secret, his alarm soared to new heights. This was the mood when the day of the masquerade party arrived. James had abandoned his idea of dressing as Ares. He was to go as a coachman instead, like Nick.

"It was the only costume they had to fit me," he said sulkily. "It robs you of your originality, Hansard, but that won't bother you as you never strove for originality in anything else."

In an effort to please Sanichton, Emma had added a shawl to her Aphrodite costume and decent kidskin slippers, in place of the sandals that revealed her toes.

"If you haven't the courage of your convictions," James said, staring disparagingly at her outfit when she came down that afternoon for a preview, "you ought to have gone as someone else. Benedict Arnold, the infamous traitor, perhaps," he sneered.

Emma peered in the mirror. "It does look horrid," she said, looking to Nick for his opinion.

"Not horrid, just—"

James supplied the word. "A hodgepodge, neither flesh nor fowl. They had a rather nice lady's Italian Renaissance costume at the shop when I was there. Something along the line of the outfit Juliet wore in the play the other night. A free-flowing gown and a copotain."

"What on earth is that?" Emma asked.

"You recall Juliet's headpiece, with a high, conical crown and a lacy thing suspended from it. Very romantic. If you hurry, it might still be there. The gown has sleeves," he added, glancing doubtfully at Emma's arms, which were naked below the shawl.

"Perhaps I should hire the outfit," she said, again looking for Nick's opinion.

"Suit yourself. My carriage is free, if you want to go and try it on."

"I shall. This girdle pinches my waist."

James resumed his reading, and Emma went abovestairs to change into a street dress. Nick went to call the carriage for her. He was relieved that James hadn't offered to take her. Miss Foxworth had volunteered to accompany her. The butler was just admitting a visitor when Nick entered the hall. Nick took him into his study, as Gertrude was in the saloon, and, so, he could not notice that James slipped quickly out of the saloon.

Chapter Eighteen

"I wish Derek were here for the party tonight," Miss Foxworth said, as the carriage took them to the costumers. "How he would love it. I wrote and told him about it, but have had no reply."

"I haven't heard from Papa for days," Emma said. A wince of guilt stabbed her. She still hadn't answered that letter. "I do hope Derek is forwarding the post."

"Your letters would have been delayed, as they have to be forwarded from Whitehern."

"Yes, that is deceitful of me. I shall write to Papa from Nick's house tomorrow and tell him I am in London. Worrying that he'll find out spoils half the fun."

"Always best to be truthful when you can," replied Miss Foxworth, who had smiled and called Emma "a sly minx" in approving accents when Emma first discussed the plan with her.

The costume shop held half a dozen customers, who were looking over the outfits. The costumes were arranged on racks according to sex, size, and quality. When Emma made her request, the clerk went immediately to the correct rack and brought out the Juliet gown. It was a fine muslin, pale gold, embroidered down the front and halfway up the wide-bottomed sleeves. Its modest fashion pleased her, and the loose style made a perfect fit unnecessary.

"Do you have the hat to go with it?" she asked. "The one with the high, pointed crown?"

The clerk removed it from a shelf behind the counter, where the various hats were kept covered in muslin against the dust.

Emma thought it looked rather foolish, and when she tried it on, it was uncomfortable besides, towering like a giant steeple above her head. She would wear it to greet the guests and remove it for the dancing. The clerk wrapped up the outfit, and Emma paid and left the shop.

She and Miss Foxworth had no sooner set foot on the street than they saw a crowd gathered on the corner and heard exclamations of alarm.

"Is he hurt bad?" one woman asked.

"Not dead, I hope?" a man exclaimed.

"Shockin' the speed these bucks drive at. Knocked the poor soul clean off his feet and didn't even bother to stop."

Emma said, "I wonder if anyone has sent for a doctor. We'd best inquire." She could spot no gentlemen in the throng and feared the crowd had gathered to gawk rather than help. The crowd parted to let the ladies through. When she got a view of the victim, she blanched. "It's James!" she cried.

Her first thought was that he had come to make mischief, but when she saw him lying in the road with blood on his forehead and his face dreadfully white, she chided herself.

She ran forward and leaned over him. "James, are you all right?" What a foolish question. He was very obviously not all right.

He was not dead, however. His eyelids fluttered open, and he gazed at her without recognition. She turned to try to discern which of the throng could be trusted to send for a doctor and was relieved to see Lord Hansard's coachman hurrying forward. She ran to him.

"Lord James has had an accident," she said. "We must get him home."

"Is he hurt bad, your ladyship?"

"I'm not sure. He didn't seem to recognize me."

The clerk who had served Emma came pelting out of the shop. He proved to be the proprietor. "Bring him inside," he said. "We can't leave the poor soul lying in the street. I've a set of rooms behind my shop."

Even as he spoke, he summoned a couple of young men in the crowd to carry James inside.

Emma said to the coachman, "You'd best send for a doctor to come here—and Lord Hansard. Hurry! It might be serious."

The coachman left, and Emma darted into the shop. The men carrying James had already disappeared through a curtained archway at the back of the room. She noticed the proprietor closing the door to the street and putting up a "Closed" sign and thought it very considerate of him.

"Where is Lord James?" she asked.

"He's in the bedroom, your ladyship."

Emma looked around for Miss Foxworth and discovered that she hadn't come in. "My friend has got locked out. Would you mind opening the door?"

"The lady in the blue pelisse?"

"Yes."

"I'll fetch her." But when he returned a moment later, it was to announce that the lady had left. Someone said she had got into a carriage.

Emma gave a sigh of exasperation. Miss Foxworth had hopped into Hansard's carriage. It was just like her. She grew faint at the sight of blood, but she might have waited in this outer room. It wasn't proper for a lady to be here unaccompanied, but at least Hansard would arrive soon.

"Very well. Take me to Lord James," she said.

"Right this way, ma'am."

She followed him through the arch, down a longish, dark corridor to a door. He tapped, but didn't wait to be let in. He opened the door, ushered Emma in, closed the door behind her, and said in a gloating voice, "Here she is." No polite "your lady-ship" or "ma'am" now.

Emma looked across the room—it was a small, shabby parlor—to see James sitting at his ease on a horsehair sofa, wiping some red coloring from his forehead. Red stage blood, or perhaps ordinary paint, from the difficulty he was having in removing it. Of the other men there was no sign. Just James and the proprietor who had brought her here, smiling triumphantly at each other.

Emma realized in a flash what James had in mind. He had made his arrangements with this Eddie, and then told her about the Juliet outfit to lure her to the shop. He couldn't close the shop, or she wouldn't have been able to get in, so he arranged that "accident." Whether Miss Foxworth had actually left was a moot point. In any case, it hardly mattered. She would not be much help, and Nick would soon be here. As she ran her mind over the street scene, she recalled that neither James nor his helper had heard her telling the coachman to send for Hansard. They thought they had an hour or more before she would be missed at Berkeley Square.

All she had to determine was whether James meant to carry her off to Gretna Green, or have his way with her without benefit of clergy. And, of course, she must delay him until Nick arrived. She set aside the costume she had been carrying and went a step closer to him.

"Well, James," she said, smiling. "I congratulate you on a remarkably speedy recovery. I'm so happy your wounds are not serious."

"It is my heart that is wounded, but it will soon be better, when I make you mine."

She sat down on a chair beside the sofa and said in a civil voice, "What, exactly, do you have in mind?"

He gave her a chiding look. "I promised Hansard that if I compromised you, I would do the right thing by you."

He looked at a decanter of wine and two glasses on the table. His eyes, at close range, betrayed a fevered glitter of excitement that suggested trickery. Emma noticed that one glass was already full. Which one had he drugged, the glass or the decanter?

"That was decent of you," she said.

"I am a gentleman. One must consider family. Can I pour you a glass of wine, my dear?"

"Thank you." He smiled smugly as he poured, and she accepted the glass. It was the decanter that was drugged, then. "I'm sure Lord Revson will be delighted at your latest escapade," she said. She raised the glass to her lips, but was careful not to take any into her mouth.

"He will! Don't think he'll get his back up at the irregular nature of our marriage, once I waltz home with a dashed heiress." He looked at her warily and added, "Though for both our sakes, it would be better if you came along quietly."

"Came along where? To Gretna Green?"

"If you like, Emma." His eyes turned to her glass, as if measuring the level of wine.

"What is the alternative?"

"We could be married in London."

"Ah, a special license, I expect?"

"Just so. I have friends in the clergy. It can easily be arranged."

"I'm surprised you haven't arranged it already." She glanced around the room in a disapproving way. "But then all your arrangements are shabby, to say the least. I'm disappointed in you, James. I had thought you would carry the thing off in better style."

"It wasn't easy, with Hansard guarding you like a hawk."

"Surely I merit a headache powder at least." She massaged her temples. "My head is splitting with all this fracas."

"Eddie will have one. You can take it with your wine," he suggested.

"Yes."

While James went to the door to call Eddie, she exchanged her glass for his. James locked the door behind him and was back in a trice; he emptied the headache powder into her glass, smiling all the while. He whirled it around until the powder began to dissolve.

"There you go, my pet," he said. "Drink it up. You'll feel better in no time." He took up the other glass.

She lifted her glass to his and clinked them together. "To our happy future," she said, and drank. James also drank.

He couldn't conceal his triumph. His voice had a gloating quality when he said, "I must say, you're rather jolly under the circumstances, Emma."

"I like a man with initiative. You haven't finished describing the alternative to Gretna Green, James. What did you have in mind?"

"You haven't finished your headache powder, Emma. Best drink it up and let the powder do its job." She lifted her glass and took a long sip. James did likewise.

"Well?" she asked. "Where is the wedding to occur?"

"I thought a small, private do at Papa's house tomorrow morning," he said.

"But where do we spend tonight?"

"At Papa's house."

"Without being married!" She thought she had better begin yawning and covered her lips in a simulated yawn, while peering to see if James was showing any signs of sleepiness. He yawned, too, and shook his head.

"If I'd thought for a moment you would be so agreeable, I would have had the license ready and got married today. But I shan't molest you tonight, Emma. That is a promise."

"Are there any servants at your Papa's house?"

"The housekeeper and one—" He shook his head in confusion. Then he peered sleepily at Emma. "What did you—"

She picked up her glass and finished her wine. "My headache is feeling much better," she said brightly, as James crumpled to a heap on the sofa.

Emma shook her head, then went to lock the door in case Eddie came to investigate. It was another fifteen minutes before the front door of the shop began trembling from Hansard's assault. Eddie came to the parlor door and called in, "There's people at the front door, Lord James. What should I do?"

"Let them in, Eddie," Emma said.

"Is Lord James all right?"

"He's fine. He says to let them in."

"Let me talk to him."

"Do as I say! Lord James is indisposed."

There was no further sound from Eddie. He knew something had gone amiss and darted out the back door, to disappear into the teeming streets of London. Emma waited a moment to make sure Eddie had left before opening the parlor door. Even as she did it, she heard the front door burst open and Hansard's loud voice calling, "Emma! James!"

Before she could answer, he was there, with his face pinched in anxiety and his eyes burning fiercely. "Emma!" he cried, and crushed her in his arms.

The absurdity of it was too much. Emma was overcome with an undignified fit of giggles, which she tried manfully to suppress. Men! James and his idiotic scheme to seduce her, Hansard rushing to rescue her from her comatose pursuer.

Hansard's lips were at her ear. His voice was tense with anxiety. "My dear, are you all right?"

The effort of choking back the laughter brought tears to her eyes. Hansard lifted his head and gazed down at her. Emma saw such concern and love in his eyes that she felt humbled. He did love her, even if he didn't know it yet. A man didn't feel that desperate anxiety for a mere friend. She melted against the warm, hard wall of his chest, as his arms held her safe in an iron grip.

Her choking laughter turned to a whimper in her throat as she met his gaze. For a long moment they looked at each other as if hypnotized. Emma's lips trembled open, just as his head lowered. She waited for his kiss, but he merely brushed his lips gently against her cheek.

"This is all my fault," he said, in a shaken voice. "If he's touched you, I'll kill the bastard." He released her and turned to look about the room. He saw James sprawled out on the sofa with the red paint smeared over his left eye.

"Is he—Did you have to—"

"That's stage paint on his forehead. He's not dead, Nick. He's drugged," she said, half sorry to have to tell him. She felt that if Nick could have been her rescuer, he might have realized he loved her.

"What happened?" he asked, reaching for the wine decanter.

"Don't drink that!" she cried. "It's drugged."

She briefly outlined what had happened. Nick listened, nodding and asking a few questions. When her story was told, he felt rather foolish, running to rescue a lady who had already rescued herself. Emma saw his mood change and tried in vain to recapture that first flame that had flared between them.

"I don't know what I would have done if you hadn't come," she said.

"I expect you would have hired a hansom cab and brought him home. I'll have John Groom help me carry him out."

"Why don't you take him to his papa's house? There are a few servants there."

"No, I'll send word to Revson to come and carry him back to Revson Hall. It's not safe to let the wretch run loose."

James was stashed on one banquette of Hansard's carriage; Nick and Emma sat on the other.

"Did Miss Foxworth get home?" Emma asked, trying for an unemotional subject.

"She arrived as I was leaving. She said she was locked out of the costume shop and didn't like to loiter about the streets alone. She found a cab to bring her, fortunately."

At Berkeley Square James was carried in by the

servants and taken up to his bedroom. Hansard beckoned Emma into his study.

"Before I write to Revson," he said, "I must know exactly what indignities you suffered at his son's hands."

"He didn't touch me. He simply planned to marry me. And I shouldn't expect too much from Revson. James tells me that his papa wouldn't care how he arranged the thing, so long as he married an heiress."

Nick shook his head. "Quite a family I planned to marry you into," he said. "That's an apology, Emma. Word of this is bound to get about. No doubt the young jackass has been boasting of this stunt to his friends. It might be as well if we leave London soon."

"Oh, yes! I am feeling so guilty about fooling Papa. I'm on tenterhooks to get back to Whitehern."

"Might as well try to enjoy the party tonight, however," he said, rather grimly. "If Sanichton comes up to scratch—" He stopped and looked at her questioningly. "I expect James's caper has made you more determined than ever to accept Sanichton?"

Emma directed a long, searching gaze at him. She read the hope and doubt and something else that might be love in his eyes.

"Would you be awfully angry with me if I didn't, after all your troubles in finding me a husband?" she asked, and smiled inwardly as his face softened with pleasure. "I fear I might find him dull after our recent adventures."

"That is entirely up to you," he said, nodding his acceptance.

"Is it, Nick?" she asked. "I still need a husband." Then before he could answer, she turned and ran upstairs, smiling.

Chapter Nineteen

Emma's Juliet costume had been left behind after the escapade at the costume shop. She had to wear the Aphrodite gown with the too tight girdle and the shawl. It seemed vain to go as the goddess of love and beauty, so she decided to leave off the diadem of stars and say she was one of the Graces. This conformed with Miss Foxworth's and Lady Gertrude's outfits. They were going as ladies from classical antiquity as well and were draped in comfortable sheets of colored muslin with crowns of vine leaves, one carrying a small amphora, the other a laurel branch.

They all wore their costumes to the family dinner. Emma had hoped James's disgrace might be kept quiet, but it was all Lady Gertrude spoke of while they ate.

"So James has lost another heiress." She glanced sadly at Emma. "I tremble to think what his papa will say when he hears the tale. He vowed not to bail James out of trouble again. I wager he will be packed off to India. He'll come home when he's old with a yellow, ravaged face." She looked hopefully to Emma, to see if this softened her up to accept the lad.

"I pity India," Nick grumbled, and jabbed at his beefsteak.

Miss Foxworth lamented again that Derek was not here to enjoy the masquerade. "How he loves a masquerade. I wager he would come as a jockey if he were here, though he's much too big, of course."

Nick remained behind alone after the meal, musing over the situation as he sipped his port. He had originally thought Emma too lowborn to bring into his family. The thought facing him now was that his family was too outrageous for her to accept. And on top of it all, it had been his own idea to bring James to Waterdown. If James had succeeded with his harebrained scheme . . . He felt a mounting anxiety that something would happen to Emma. A sleeping draft didn't last forever. He'd have to warn Emma and the servants to be alert this evening. He set aside his glass and went to join the ladies. His eyes flew to Emma. Only when he saw her safely wedged between the two older ladies did he draw a level breath.

Before long the group went to the hall to begin welcoming the guests. Nick and his aunt Gertrude greeted them and passed them along to Emma and Miss Foxworth, who led them to the ballroom. He had arranged only a small party of thirty couples, but they came in an amazing variety of costumes. Two of the first to arrive were Sanichton and his sister. Lady Margaret was dressed as a shepherdess in a panniered skirt that showed six inches of muslin underleggings and flat slippers with big gilt buckles. She wore a leghorn bonnet with streaming blue ribbons and carried a gilded shepherd's staff. It was an unfortunate choice of outfit for a tall, rather severe lady. She looked like a mama dressed up in her daughter's clothes.

But her costume was nothing to compare with her brother's for ludicrousness. To show Emma his light side, Sanichton had taken the unfortunate notion to come rigged out as a court jester in cap and bells. A close-fitting top and tights in parti-color, harlequin

170

hues completed his ensemble. A Lord James might have carried off the ridiculous outfit, but a dignified Lord Sanichton didn't know what to do with it. He blushed, ill at ease and feeling every bit as foolish as he looked.

"You are in fetching form, Emma," he said. "Came as a—a lady, I see," he said, puzzling over the outfit.

"Yes, I am in disguise from my true nature," she joked.

Sanichton even realized it was a joke, but no witty retort came to mind. "Oh, but I meant a foreign lady of some sort," he said. Then quickly changed the subject. "Ah, Hansard, I mistook you for a mail-coach driver. Heh heh."

"Then my disguise has succeeded," Nick said, feeling sorry for him.

"And Maggie has come as a shepherdess," Sanichton said.

"Charming," Nick lied, giving Lady Margaret's hand a shake.

The guests continued streaming in. It seemed that Nick's guests were quite tired of their silks and satins and diamonds. Fine lords came as lamplighters and Smithfield drovers, one even dressing as a fireman. Another wore a white tail wig and the red jacket and blue waistcoat of a Chelsea pensioner. Miss Allyson came decked out as a shrimper in a muslin cap, short-sleeved shirt, and old tattered skirt. Lady Angela Strathmore was disguised as a seller of hot cross buns, carrying a basket of her wares. Her husband was outfitted as a baker in a white apron and leggings, with flour powdering his hair and face.

Those who were not tired of finery came decked out in grander habiliments. There was a royal herald, a judge, a general, and two admirals. They had all come to enjoy themselves, and before long the dancing was in full swing. Masks, baskets, staffs, and other cumbersome paraphernalia were set aside to allow greater freedom of movement. Through it all Emma kept one eye on the door to see if James appeared, and another on Nick, hoping to see him coming toward her. He, too, was concerned about James and could pay her little attention, except to look often in her direction to see she was safe in the ballroom.

Nick's fears were not in vain. Around eleven o'clock James appeared at the doorway. When he had realized the stunt Emma had played on him, he sank in shame. He had decided to show his remorse—and hopefully secure her silence—by literally donning sackcloth and ashes and apologizing. That should satisfy Hansard, and save him from his papa's retribution. Lord Revson was not quite so lenient in his views on winning a bride as James had indicated.

The cotillion was just ending when Emma happened to glance at Nick. She saw him stiffen and hasten toward the door. A glance showed her why. She excused herself to her partner and ran after him, arriving as Nick was dragging James down the hall to his study. Emma managed to slip in before Nick kicked the door shut and turned in wrath on his cousin.

"You have the gall to show your nose after that stunt you tried this afternoon!" he exclaimed. "And rigged out like a scarecrow."

James hung his head humbly. "I come in peace, Cousin," he said. "Do you not recognize sackcloth and ashes when you see them? Your cook was kind enough to lend me her potato bag and the cinder box from the stove. I am performing public penance for my wrongs."

Nick was speechless. James spoke on, turning his ash-covered face to Emma. "I apologize most humbly,

Lady Capehart, and give you my solemn promise that I shall pester you no more. I adore the ground you walk on, but I could never marry a lady who is more clever than I. I sense you are the sort who would search out all her lord's picayune secrets, who would rifle pockets and go calling on her husband's light-skirts."

"You read me like a book, James."

"So I feared, but I trust we can still be friends. After a few months with Sanichton, you will be glad for a friend like me."

"I wouldn't have you for a friend if I were married to Jack Ketch." She looked at Nick and shook her head. "I take leave to tell you, Lord Hansard, your cousin is incorrigible."

"Ah, no," James said sadly. "*You* could have corrected my little ways, had you considered it worth your while, Emma. But then I rather like me as I am. Adieu, my love. One dance, and I shall return to my room to wash off these ashes. They begin to itch."

"You're not going into the ballroom dressed like that," Nick declared.

"Would it be possible to look more ridiculous than Sanichton? I shouldn't think he would be so eager to announce to Society that Emma has made a fool of him."

"I've promised Sanichton the waltzes," Emma said. "I really ought to go. They'll be starting any moment."

"I shall watch from the doorway, my last view of you, my beloved, in his arms. What a dreadful mistake you are making, Emma. But you will be mine soon enough. You will make a better mistress than wife, I think."

"And you would make a better—*anything* than a husband," she retorted, and left.

Emma regretted she had promised the waltzes to Sanichton. He had never seemed less appealing than he did that evening, when he tried to make himself agreeable by being frivolous. His cap and bells did not become him. She liked him better as a prude. But she wouldn't satisfy James by showing her displeasure. He had come to gaze at her forlornly from the doorway, as promised.

"By Jove, this is something like," Sanichton said with feigned heartiness, as he waltzed sedately around the floor, bells jingling from the tails of his cap. "Er, your shawl is slipping, Emma. Wouldn't want everyone gaping at your bare arms."

"Is something wrong with my arms?" she asked pertly.

"No, not really. They're very nice arms."

He wanted to deliver a mild lecture, but he also wanted to compliment Emma and show her his dashing, cavalier side. Unfortunately, he found it hard to talk and dance at the same time, especially with Lord James glowering like a gargoyle from the doorway. Before long James espied a pretty shrimp woman not dancing and invaded the ballroom to accost Miss Allyson. Emma was relieved he had found a new victim.

"Relax, Horatio," she said. "It's a party, not a wake."

"Let us slip out for a minute, Emma. There is something I want to ask you. I can't do it here."

She knew what the something was and felt that the sooner it was over with, the better. A life with Sanichton was impossible. She would refuse gently, assuring him that he was much too good for her.

"Very well," she said, and allowed him to waltz her out the door—into the arms of her papa and Aunt Hildegarde.

Chapter Twenty

Having spent the day on the road, Mr. Milmont and his sister had not changed into evening clothes. He was a large man with black hair silvering at the temples to add to his considerable dignity. He stood like Jehovah, with a thundercloud on his dark visage. His black eyes burned like coals as he stared at his wayward daughter. As he had advanced in years, his eyebrows had sprouted into two tufts that added to his menacing aspect. He always wore black jackets. He considered colors frivolous.

Hildegarde was more lenient in that respect. She permitted herself the indulgence of a dun-colored pelisse that matched her complexion and had the added advantage of not showing the dust.

The unwitting butler had admitted the pair, mistaking them for late-arriving guests. He had not even bothered to call Lord Hansard. Aunt Hildegarde stood beside her brother, her long nose pinched in delighted wrath as she surveyed the throng in the ballroom.

"So this is how you carry on behind our backs!" she exclaimed. "Consorting with dustmen and fishmongers and every sort of lowlife."

"Papa! How did you get here?" Emma exclaimed.

"When you failed to reply to my letter, Hildegarde

and I felt it incumbent on us to undertake the arduous trip to Whitehern."

"We felt you must be ill," Hildegarde added. "Mr. Hunter, the beau you left behind at Whitehern, directed us here. And this, I collect, would be the caper merchant who calls himself Lord Hansard?" she said, turning a fiery eye on poor Lord Sanichton.

"Indeed no," Emma exclaimed.

"I thought not!" Hildegarde cried in triumph. "It is all a hum, Milmont. She hired the house herself, to flaunt her body with this assortment of riffraff. I told you you shouldn't have left her alone at Whitehern all that time, with too much money and no one to look after her."

"I assure you, Papa, it is nothing of the sort! It is only a little masquerade party."

The mention of such licentiousness was like pouring oil on the fire of Hildegarde's wrath. "A masquerade party, and poor John not yet cold in his grave."

"He's been buried for eighteen months," Emma pointed out.

"I say!" Lord Sanichton said, putting a protective arm around Emma. Always alive to propriety, he whispered to her, "It might be best to continue this discussion in private."

Several of the guests had heard the argument at the door and were staring curiously. James happened to glance in that direction. Seeing Emma's troubled expression, he abandoned the shrimp woman and darted toward her. He smiled blandly at Milmont and Hildegarde.

"What intriguing outfits," he said. "No, don't tell me! It's on the tip of my tongue. Now I have it. You're Saints—members of Wilberforce's zealous reform sect. What is it called?"

Milmont and Hildegarde were momentarily struck

speechless by such insolence from what looked like a dustman.

"Clapham Sect," replied Sanichton, who subscribed to the *Christian Observer*.

"Come along, Wilber, I'll find you a pretty wench," James said, and put his hand on Milmont's elbow.

Milmont shook him off as if he were a small but tenacious pup. "Who is this whelp, Emma?" he demanded.

James, bridling at this treatment, lifted his chin and replied waggishly, "I'm His Highness's whelp at Kew. Pray tell me, sir, whose dog are you?"

"Pay him no heed, Papa. He is a great joker," Emma said. "This is Lord James Philmore of Revson Hall."

Milmont looked at the potato bag and dirty face and replied, "And I'm the king of England." So saying, he pushed James aside to grab Emma's arm.

"You're mad enough to be!" James said, with an impertinent smile around the little group at this riposte.

Sensing that James was inciting the guests to greater wrath, Sanichton intervened. "If you'll just step along, sir, the study is right down the hall," he said to Milmont.

"I don't take orders from a clown in my own daughter's house," Milmont said, and flung Sanichton aside.

"You have some explaining to do, young lady," Hildegarde said, shaking a finger under Emma's nose. "Flaunting your body half naked in public."

The butler realized his error in having admitted the couple and ran to fetch Lord Hansard, who had gone to his study to take a headache powder. "It seems I've accidentally admitted a couple of gentry folks who weren't invited, your lordship," he said.

"I'm flattered. I didn't think my party was grand enough to encourage illicit entry. Are they causing trouble?"

"I fear so, your lordship. I could put them out, but they appear to know Lady Capehart. Her ladyship calls the gentleman 'Papa.' "

Hansard froze like a statue. "Good lord! Milmont!" he said in a weak voice.

"That's the name he gave, and a Miss Hildegarde Milmont."

Without another word Hansard shot out the door and down the corridor, just as James was shoving Mr. Milmont against the wall. To be fair, Mr. Milmont had shoved him first.

"James!" Hansard roared, in a voice that caused every head in his ballroom to swivel toward the doorway.

"These yahoos are insulting Emma, Cuz," James said. "The old bint called her a hurly-burly girl."

"If you'd please step along into the saloon," Nick said to the Milmonts, with a wary glance at the staring faces in the ballroom. Dancing had virtually ceased, though the music continued uncertainly.

Hildegarde looked at the red jacket on Nick, the blue cuffs and brass buttons. "Are you hiring out rooms to the mail-coach drivers on top of the rest?" she demanded of her niece.

"This is Lord Hansard, Auntie," Emma said. "This is his disguise for the masquerade party. He most assuredly does not drive the stage."

The name Lord Hansard was familiar to Hildegarde from Emma's letters. Derek Hunter had told them Emma was staying in London with Lord Hansard. They knew him to be John's neighbor and friend. They also knew him to be an extremely eligible *parti* of good character. Hildegarde had been impressed with the neighborhood and the house when they approached it. The butler, too, seemed like a proper butler. Even the accents of the clown and the dustman (for so she considered Sanichton and James) were the effete accents of the nobility. She accepted that they were who they said they were. Mr. Milmont was slower to assimilate these suggestive items.

Hildegarde could not rip up at a lord. She had to take her ill temper out on her niece. "A fine spectacle you are making of yourself, Emma. What will Lord Hansard think of you?"

"But the party was his idea!" Emma said, looking helplessly at Nick.

"It's no good blaming your hoydenish ways on others. An adult accepts blame for her own doings. It was John who spoiled you. Too soft by half," she added, forgetting that the blame was only Emma's.

"I take leave to tell you, Mrs. Wilberforce," James said, "there is not a soft bone in Emma's body. She is steel to the marrow. Did she not this very day rescue herself when I abducted her? Tell her, Emma."

"It's Miss Milmont, James," Emma said.

"Abducted!" Hildegarde shrieked, and drew out her hartshorn. "Ruined. You're ruined, child. There is nothing so ill-bred as being abducted. No decent gentleman will ever have you now."

"Rubbish," James said. "She is as good as engaged to Lord Sanichton. You won't find a more upright bore in all of London."

Nick cast a commanding eye at Sanichton, who stared at Emma as if the scales had just fallen from his eyes, and he beheld the scarlet face of shame and degradation. He still loved her body, but a young lady who allowed herself to be abducted, and who came saddled with such a family as this besides, was really too much for him to contemplate marrying. He liked peace and quiet in his life. There would be no peace with Emma. She drew chaos as the flame draws the moth.

Hildegarde looked at Sanichton consideringly. She saw the reluctance on his silly face. She was not one of those who disliked to say, "I told you so!" She said it with relish, "I told you so! No decent man—"

Nick stepped forward and put a hand on Emma's arm. "You are mistaken, ma'am," he said. "I have this very day asked Emma to marry me."

"My sister said no *decent* man," Mr. Milmont said, glowering. "This is the sort of scarecrow you will end up with and deserve, Emma. A mail-coach driver."

"No, no, Milmont," Hildegarde said, rather urgently. "He really *is* Lord Hansard." Disappointment warred with glee in her bosom. "I told you so," were hard words to eat, yet to claim kinship to a marquess proved a tasty sauce! "Emma?" she said, rather commandingly.

Emma stared at Hansard, trying to read his mood. When she said nothing, but simply stared at him with a question in her dark eyes, he took her hand in his. "And she has done me the honor to accept," he added firmly, squeezing her fingers.

"Is this true, Emma?" Mr. Milmont asked hopefully.

"Are you calling Lord Hansard a liar?" was James's unhelpful comment.

"Of course it's true, Papa," Emma said in a trembling voice.

"The masquerade is our engagement party," Nick said. "You will not want to join the dancers without a costume, but perhaps you will help us celebrate with a glass of champagne—in the saloon."

He feared champagne might be on their interdict list, but for such an occasion they accepted.

"Perhaps just one glass, to celebrate," Hildegarde said in a whole new voice. The Marchioness of Hansard! What a coup! And he was young, too. He would accomplish what Sir John had not—give Emma children to settle her down.

Lord Sanichton had slipped quietly away during the discussion. Lord James, however, who enjoyed any sort of imbroglio, tagged along, leaving a trail of ashes on the marble floor and Persian carpet. Nick led the group into his saloon, whose grandeur removed any lingering doubts as to his character. A man with such fine furnishings as the room held was obviously honorable. The old paintings on the wall alone were sponsor enough. Nick asked his butler to bring the wine and glasses.

To pass the time until the wine arrived, he said, "I hope you will do me the honor to stay here with me overnight. You won't want to be going to a hotel at this hour."

"Very obliging of you, milord," Hildegarde said, then smirked.

"Who has been chaperoning you, Emma?" Milmont asked, but he asked it in a pleasant tone, not accusingly.

"Miss Foxworth," she said. Then as she recalled her papa's views of that dame, she added, "And Lady Gertrude, Nick's aunt."

"I should adore to meet her," Hildegarde said, and smiled. "But we shan't interrupt your little party, Lord Hansard. Tomorrow will be soon enough."

The wine came and was drunk while they discussed the details of the marriage.

"If the wedding is to take place soon, we can stay for it," Hildegarde said hopefully.

"Actually, we plan to be married at Waterdown, Nick's country place," Emma said. She feared Nick

181

had only proposed to save her from her family's ire. Delaying the wedding until an excuse could be found to terminate the engagement, if that was his wish, was the least she could do.

"How soon?" Miss Milmont asked eagerly.

"Next autumn," Emma replied. "Nick is very busy just now with political business. The prime minister quite depends on him." Hildegarde smiled fondly. She could not object to the delay when the cause was so high in Society. "He won't be free for a honeymoon until the end of September."

She trusted four months was too long for her papa to stay away from home.

"I hope you don't plan to stay here in London that long," Hildegarde said. "A few days' visit with your fiancé is unexceptionable, but to virtually move into his house—"

"Oh no! I shall be returning to Whitehern very soon."

"The doctor thought the change would be good for Miss Foxworth's cold. And the noise of replacing the roof, you know, was hard on her nerves," Nick added. Then he recalled that the Milmonts had been at Whitehern and no repairs were in progress.

"I saw no signs of the workmen," Mr. Milmont mentioned.

"They're doing a little job for me at the moment," Hansard said, without blinking. "Emma was kind enough to allow them to interrupt the work on her roof to do my conservatory roof, as it was leaking rather badly. In fact, that is how we came to—to become engaged," he said.

"How romantic!" Hildegarde sighed.

James looked at her askance. "Love on a rooftop? It sounds highly dangerous. Take care you don't fall, Nick."

"I cannot think they were actually *on* the roof, Lord James," Hildegarde chided gently. "But then you are a jokesmith. I recognized your little poem about His Highness's dog. Alexander Pope, I believe. So clever. A great pity he was so deformed."

"Was it Pope? He does not usually resort to doggerel. A pun! How clever of me."

Hildegarde frowned in confusion. Puns, or any sort of levity, were completely foreign to her. Besides, the unaccustomed wickedness of champagne was making her sleepy. She soon began yawning behind her fingers, and she and Mr. Milmont were shown abovestairs to chambers that gave them an even higher regard for their new in-law to be. Nick had whispered to his butler to remove the French paintings of nudes from the green and blue guest chambers and replace them with landscapes, and had dallied along the way until the switch could be accomplished.

Chapter Twenty-one

A midnight supper was being served when Emma and Nick rejoined the party.

"I'm sorry, Nick," Emma said. "Naturally we shall find some excuse to break the engagement before September." She waited on nettles to see if he agreed.

"We'll talk about it later. We must return to our guests and make some excuse for that interlude in the hall. Everyone will be wondering."

Emma was left in doubt as to his intentions. Surely he would have said something if he truly wanted to marry her.

James had preceded them to the supper room. To atone for his abduction of Emma, he had told everyone that a pair of lunatics had escaped from Bedlam and found their way to Hansard's door. The story was so well circulated that it proved impossible to scotch. Only Lord Sanichton knew the truth, and he was so ashamed at not having stood up for Emma that he pretended to believe it.

It was two o'clock before the last guest left.

"Now we can have that chat," Nick said, taking Emma's hand and leading her to the saloon.

During the long supper, Nick had paid her scarcely any heed. He was too busy talking away the intrusion of the uninvited guests. Emma had come to the conclusion that her father and her aunt, if not her own behavior, had given Nick a disgust of her. Her shoulders sagged from the fatigue of feigning merriment.

"If I had ever dreamed it would turn out like this I would have accepted Derek's offer," she said. "Nothing could be as bad as this."

Nick studied her pale face, which was heavy with regret. "You're hard on me, Emma. I assure you I have no notion of turning Whitehern into a stud farm."

"I don't mean that. You were splendid, Nick. A complete hand." A wistful smile tugged at her lips. "Did you see Aunt Hildegarde stare when she realized you really are a lord?"

"I was too busy watching you wilt."

"And Sanichton. What a takein. And the curious thing is that we were just on our way to the saloon for him to propose."

Nick studied her quietly, with a dark, penetrating gaze. "What answer did you intend to give him?"

"I meant to tell him we would not suit. He was much too good for me. And so are you," she said, smiling softly at him. "We shall let Papa and Aunt Hildegarde go home before we break if off. If we don't make any formal announcement, there is no reason your friends need ever know." She watched for his reaction, but saw only a gathering frown.

"I don't give a tinker's curse what my friends think."

"It would be embarrassing for you to be jilted—but not so embarrassing as being married to someone like me."

"Emma," he chided, taking her hand and lifting it to his lips. "Don't speak of yourself in such unflattering terms."

"It's true. I'm horrid. I have no notion how to go on in Society."

"Yet despite your provincial ways, everyone likes you."

"Well, they accept me, so long as I bring John's estate with me. But that's not the worst of it. I've been lying to Papa and chasing after a husband when John is—"

"Is long dead and buried. Any young lady in your position would do the same thing. I abetted you in the lies to your papa, and now that I've met him, I feel we were justified. He is overly strict. Don't feel guilty, Emma. It's natural to want to be married and have a family. I want it myself."

"And now I've thrown this obstacle in your path!"

"I don't consider an engagement to the lady I love an obstacle to marriage. Quite the contrary."

Emma looked at him with a questioning gaze, which slowly turned to trembling joy as she realized he was serious. "The lady you—love?" she asked in a whisper.

"With all my heart, for as long as I've known you. I'm a demmed fool. If I hadn't got on my high horse when you offered for me—"

"Oh Nick, don't remind me of that humiliating evening."

"But did you mean it? Did you want to marry me?"

She caught his gaze and held it. "I wouldn't have asked you if I didn't," she said simply.

"You mentioned a marriage of convenience . . ."

A spark of remembered anger flashed in her eyes, making her look more like the Emma he loved. "An inconvenient marriage, I should have said. As if I'd be satisfied with that. I only said it after you turned me down flat. Naturally I couldn't let you think I really cared."

"Naturally," he said, chewing back a smile at her frankness. "Now that we have got that cleared up ... Emma, I do want to marry you." He drew her into the circle of his arms, and she went without protesting.

She peered up at him with trusting eyes. "Do you really, Nick? You're not saying it to be kind?"

"Where did you get the absurd idea I'm kind? I'm saying it because it's true."

She tossed caution to the wind and threw her arms around his neck. "It took you long enough to realize it!"

"I've known it for ages now," he said. "I just didn't know I knew it." The last words were muffled as he crushed her against him and lowered his lips to hers for a scorching kiss. The vague discontent he had felt when Emma first showed an interest in James, his new dislike for Sanichton—all had become crystal clear. It was jealousy, plain and simple, and he hadn't even recognized it. But at least he recognized love when he held it in his arms. The swelling joy, the fierce protective instinct, the sense of rightness that filled him as the kiss deepened to passion could only be love.

It was some time later that she sat with her head on his shoulder, with Nick running his fingers through her silky curls. They were talking and laughing over their strange romance.

"If we married soon, your papa and aunt could attend the wedding without having to make a return journey," he suggested.

"I would like that," she admitted shyly. "I have been feeling so wretched about all my dishonesty with Papa. He doesn't mean to be so—" She couldn't find words for his particular brand of interference. "He is only interested in my welfare. Would you mind terribly?"

"I would like it. You can't jettison family, whatever their shortcomings. For myself, I think he did a fine job of raising his daughter."

"I told them you're busy at Whitehall," she said, and looked to Nick for a solution to this little problem.

"But if Lord Liverpool should catch a cold, then we could have a week to ourselves."

"They won't stay long if we are leaving for our honeymoon. They'll want to see Waterdown, so that Hildegarde can boast to all her friends."

"I'll have a few footmen go up to your roof to lend credence to the roof story."

Emma turned an adoring smile on her fiancé. "You think of everything, Nick. I'm so glad you accepted my offer—at last."

"Someone has to keep you in line," he murmured, and kissed her again.